Daughters
of the Oak

Includes the novella
The Manningtree Account

Paranormal Gothic Horror

-

BECKY WRIGHT

Published by Platform House
www.platformhousepublishing.com

ISBN: 9781544861449

Book & Cover Design © by Platform House
www.platformhousepublishing.com

All books by the author

Novels

The Oliver Hardacre Series
PRIORY - book 1
LORE - book 2 - coming 2022

Mr Stoker & I
Daughters of the Oak
Remember to Love Me

Novellas

The Manningtree Account
The Final Act of Mercy Dove

To my James,
for your endless love and support.

To my children,
for your love and infinite belief.

To my family & friends,
for your boundless encouragement.

A Note for the Reader

Being born in Essex and raised in Suffolk, the history of the infamous Matthew Hopkins, Witchfinder General, has always intrigued, schooling my dark fascination.

Daughters of the Oak is in no way a factual report of one of his actual witch trials, rather the spirit behind the story. I've applied poetic licence throughout the book, using this grim period of English history as the essence at the heart of this fictional tale.

However, please bear in mind, although the story I weave is fictitious, the man behind the witch hunts was very real. It is well documented how hundreds of innocent women were persecuted, tortured, and even executed at his hand, so the fate of my characters could well parallel those of real individuals. To emphasise this point, I have purposely left those condemned women nameless.

A Little History

Matthew Hopkins appeared from seemingly nowhere around 1644. There is scarce knowledge of his early years, with little documentation. However, it is thought that he was born around 1619 - 1620, the fourth child of six, to James Hopkins, a Puritan Minister of Great Wenham, Suffolk, with some records pertaining to the Minister still in existence.

It is suspected that he had been a practising Lawyer somewhere in Essex. Maybe, with little success, as with some family inheritance, he purchased The Thorn Inn in Mistley, Manningtree. It was here that he conducted his witch trials.

With the English Civil War raging across an unsettled country, superstition was rife. With his self-titled status of Witchfinder General, he scoured East Anglia. During this dark period of English history, between the years of 1644 – 1646, it is thought that the numbers of those executed by his hand could be as high as 230.

A famous witch trial of 1645 in Bury St. Edmunds, Suffolk, saw a mass hanging of 18 people in one day. Matthew Hopkins was prolific and at the centre of this trial. A second witch trial in Bury St. Edmunds in 1662 is said to have set precedence for the infamous Salem Witch Trials at the end of the century.

Matthew Hopkins disappeared from public notoriety around the end of 1646. He died of tuberculosis and was buried in Mistley, Manningtree, 12th August 1647, a young man in his late twenties.

England 1645

Civil War clutches the country in a merciless embrace. It has been raging, trudging its heavy boots, sweeping the weary nation with fear and battle, for nigh on three years.

The hearts of men, divided, The Royalists of King Charles I and Cromwell's Parliamentarians. Steadfast in their intentions, to retain or gain power, each loyal to their cause, but in fear and severe hatred of those with other, contentious ideals.

Yet, in the souls of the lowly countrymen, the humble farmer, the timid maiden, from clerk to clergy, another war rages, fuelled by ignorance. Superstition. It rules with a fierce rod. God-fearing folk seek refuge in pure beliefs and be damned any who step outside the boundary.

Parliament propaganda whispers in men's ears - There be evil. Slowly, gradually, gaining momentum 'til it spreads like wildfire. Weed out the Crown's servants of Satan. Reap the country bare of its demons. Beelzebub lurks, preying on the weak and needy. Innocent hearts to contaminate, milk to sour, butter to spoil, crops to rot.

However, there is a man. One who wheedles his employment of local parish, town, village, and hamlet. One who is trusted, esteemed, and feared. He comes, with those in his employ, to watch, gathering evidence and confession. His success speaks of a countryside rife with evil, an intemperate plague of witches, the Devil's Whores.

'Thou shall not suffer a witch to live.' Exodus 22:18

Chapter One

'Superstition reeks foul in righteous hearts.'

Manningtree - March 1645

What was it about this skittish pest that twisted her belly and quivered her skin? With brittle legs, it scuttled hither and thither. Vulnerable, fragile, yet so unaware, and so tempting.

It darted across her bare toes, halting, with one spindly limb resting upon her foot.

Foolish girl, 'tis thy turn.

Take heed, little spider, I shall tear, rip legs from thy body, one by one.

The tip of its sinewy leg tapped her bare skin. It was taunting her. Jeering, spiteful, hateful. Her fingers itched to bend, seize, clutch it, steal it up into her palms. To grip 'til it stilled.

It be thy turn, little pup.

Hush spider, or I will crush thee.

†

They had crept soundlessly. Halted on the boundary of the cottage and waited to make their claim. And claimed they had, as the glow of morning sung above the thatch. With thunderous bellows and thumping clubs, they had flogged the door and breached the sanctuary of her home.

With the sun harsh and low on the rooftops, the young maiden had been yanked, screaming, from the clutches of her kin. Her shoulders still bore the purple bruises from her sister's desperate grip. Pulled along the lane, her feet

1

dragging, trenching through the thick mud, her mother wailing in her wake.

She had resisted. She had fought. But they had been of mighty conviction and fearful intent, those men loyal to his name.

She knew not of where she was. A whirlwind of turmoil and fear had clouded her eyes as they hauled her into a room. Only now did she glance, gathering her bearings, cold, dark. The small, leaded window granted little of the early light.

An old woman stood before her, two more, younger, to either side.

Her head whipped, searching the room, eagerly hunting for something, someone familiar. She needed to claim her innocence, to free this absurd, vicious charge from her person, clear her name. How could anyone, friend or foe, see her accused of such atrocities.

There had been a misunderstanding; she wanted her to go home to her mother, to be in her bed. Mother would make it right; she always did.

A man stepped forward in the dim light. His eyes lingered on her face. He was staring, and she hated it; spiteful words always followed such glaring eyes. His face stern, creased with suspicion, he said nothing, instead gestured to the women.

With a wave of his hand, the three set upon her, tearing, ripping cloth from skin. With a strange eagerness, they grabbed like fevered dogs, fingers gouging as they tore off her bodice and skirts.

Frozen in fear and humiliation, the maiden stood in just her meagre slip.

'All of it!' he bellowed, deep, gruff. 'Strip her . . . I need to see all her flesh.'

Her arms folded about her breasts, trembling, eyes wide, staring, as the old woman pulled at her limbs, snatching them away. They were rough hands, fingers hard and callous, nails sharp and jagged. Grabbing the ribbons, she tugged at the ties, knotting them in her rage. Impatient, uncaring, unfeeling, the woman tore open the slip, exposing the maiden's breasts.

Naked, her dignity thrown to the floor with her ripped slip, an arm covering her breasts, the other desperate to conceal her virtue. Shivering, weeping, the disbelief that swamped her soul evident on her face, but they cared not.

The other women disappeared, leaving the older and the man.

'Please, I beg thee.'

'Quiet, girl,' his voice, a touch lower than before.

A lash to her cheek. 'Quiet.' The woman spat as her hand left her reddened face.

She could do nothing, shocked by the sudden pain.

'Now,' he began, calmer still.

The woman dragged a chair across the stone floor. The maiden watched her limp, her leg slightly bowed, her deformed foot lagging.

The man sat.

The maiden stood, terrified, of what, she could not decipher, her vulnerability, stark and raw, her body freezing, naked, or that he was a man. His eyes, lingering far too long, on what he should not. Heat rushed her body as panic washed over her: her heart, a deafening thump in her skull.

'Does thou know why thou are here?'

She knew not what to say, so resigned to remain silent. Merely stared with tear-soaked eyes.

He edged nearer on the chair, leaning closer, his breath brushing her skin. She wanted to move, to run. But, alas, her feet were solid on the stone floor, legs quivering, arms clutching tighter still around her body.

'Show me thy hands.'

3

She hesitated. The man held out his palms up, offering. She glanced down, confused. Compassion? No.

'Show me thy hands.'

Tentatively, she held them out, shaking. Painfully, her nipples hardened as the frigid air rushed her bare breasts. A silent prayer beneath her breath, pleading for mercy. He groaned, taking her hands, turning them over in his.

With morning light gaining. A small shard cast across his arm. Pulling her forward into it, he inspected further. Rubbing his thumbs across her wrists, he pressed. She wanted to pull away, to run, to hide. Dropping one hand, he lifted her arm, painfully twisting it, turning her. Whilst his grip tightened around her wrist, his other hand ran up her arm, around her shoulder, dragging it down her back, the curve of her hip, then under to her breast. His hand scuffed over them, halting on her nipples. She yelped with pain, fear, shame.

'Please . . .'

The old woman limped forward, gripping the maiden's arms, pushing them above her head. 'Be quiet.'

'Please?' she wept, searching the old woman's eyes for the merest speck of humanity.

'Hush. Please, girl.'

For a moment, her poor heart faltered. Her eyes urged. But her arms tugged higher, old eyes stared back, cold.

With eager hands and scanning features, the man rubbed over the delicate skin, grazing and scuffing with his nails. Suddenly, discarding her arms, the old woman stopped, crumpled to her knees, and clasped the maiden's ankles. She pushed her feet apart.

'What have I done? Please.'

The old woman looked up at the girl, her eyes suddenly flashed, with an expression the maiden could only hope to decipher, 'twas not of kindness, but, more of her own despair.

'I have no understanding, I beseech thee.'

'Enough!'

The bellow came with a great wave of his hand; it lashed across her breasts. Sitting back, he sighed.

'Thou must be quiet,' he clucked his tongue on the roof of his mouth and smiled. 'Unless thou are ready to confess?' He raised his brows in question, shaking his head with a smirk. 'Thought not.'

A faint sob beneath her breath was all she could muster; disgrace and terror had possession of her senses, her mind a whirl of bewilderment.

The woman's callous fingers continued; they ran up the inside of her legs, pushing her knees apart. The maiden began to shake, her body quivering, cowering, as the old woman rubbed her hands up her thighs, skimming the tenderness of her womanhood.

Darkness was falling over her soul, the light she had known, now tainted with hate—a nightmare. With eyes clenched tight, she drifted, taking her thoughts with her on a loving journey of escape. Feeling the warmth of morning as it crept through her window, she watched as it played on the leaded panes, seeping into her room. Heard the softness of her mother's voice as she cooked by the fire. She could smell home.

With a harsh grip on her buttocks, she swung around, eyes flying open, to see the tangible horror before her.

He rested back on the chair, his hands folded in his lap, settled on the dark knees of his breeches. She gazed, mesmerised, his fingers knitted together. Bewildered, lost in her own thoughts, she counted his digits as they unravelled. They left his knees and took her hands. She stared at her pale fingers in his rough, worn, old hands, weathered and dark. Dark like his soul.

'This can all be over. Simply confess thy sins. Confess and name thy cohorts.'

No words left her lips. Somehow, she could find none, none to answer such ridiculous requests. Confess to what? What could these people possibly imagine was the reasoning behind this play. This act of hatred and confusion. How could any of this day be anything but some bizarre performance?

'Thou shall confess. Thou has my word on that. The matter only to be if it shall be now or later.' He sat back on the chair, almost tossing her hand, causing her to stagger until her back hit the rough wall.

'Thou has nothing to say?'

'I know not.'

'Confess, girl. Confess the evil that has sodden thy soul.'

Abruptly, he stood, grasping the back of the chair, hands gripping tight, rage emanating from his face. With a violent rush, he lunged, his fist making harsh contact with the maiden's face.

Shocked, horrified, the pain drew the air from her lungs as fire burnt her cheek. Her tender skin tore. Blood spurted and spattered, blurring her vision. She clutched her face, burying it in her hands.

Instinctively, she wanted to scream, yell, sob. Instead, restoring the air to her lungs in a sharp gasp, she dropped her hands, her face resolute. She glared, unblinking, as the blinding pain silently scorched every nerve ending.

Adamant, with gritted teeth, the maiden shook her head.

'Are thou ready to confess?'

'I do not understand.' With a quavering voice, the words splintered and fractured. 'I am not a witch.'

He grumbled, a deep rumble in his chest, shaking his head in annoyance.

'I see.'

Once again, he raised his fist. Impulsively, she cowered, bringing her arms up, wrapping them around her head. As she stooped over, folding her body in protection, his knee rose. With peremptory drive, it smashed into her face. Her nose exploded in a crimson torrent.

She collapsed to the stone floor. Great wailing screams left her lungs. The pain binding her in its pitiful prison of agony.

'If thou are sure.'

'Wait.'

'Thou are ready to announce thy dealings with the devil?'

'Please, I beseech thee. I am innocent.'

'He predicted as much.' With raised brows, he grabbed the chair, taking it with him; upon reaching the door, he turned. 'He shall be here soon enough. I urge thee to confess.'

'Wait, please.' Her mind whirled in muddled, clouded. She dragged herself up, trying to stand, her knees hard on the stone floor, hands clutching at the wall. 'Please . . . who?

'Him. The General.'

'General?'

'The Witchfinder, himself.' Laughter left his lips in a drip of venom.

'I am not a witch.'

'Of course, is that not what a witch would say, to plead innocence?'

'It is the truth.'

Sliding back down, her head thudded against the wall.

He hesitated with a hand resting on the doorknob, carefully placing the chair on the floor, and strode back.

She was hunched, a thin, bare figure of young womanhood, her pretty face, torn, smashed, blood smeared. Her eyes would not open. She heard his footsteps and recoiled. Gently, his hand stroked her hair, easing the dark strands to reveal the bruised mess of her face.

The maiden froze as he caressed her cheek. Wiping his thumb across the open wounds. Smearing his fingers over her cheek as a fresh rush of blood oozed. He dragged his fingernails, raking them through the raw flesh. She whimpered.

'Such a pretty face, once,' he whispered in her ear as his hands wove into her hair. 'He shall not be as tolerant as I.'

He glared, pulling her head back to meet his.

Powerless, her eyes remained clenched shut. The pain, excruciating. Clutching, knotting his fingers through her crimson smeared hair, he pulled. Dragging her body up, grazing her bare skin against the abrasive wall. Her slender limbs lashed, tugging at his hands.

She hung there. Her bare toes scarcely touching the floor. Her eyes now wide, traumatised, stupefied. She could see only hatred.

He smiled. 'Now? Or would thou rather endure more? I guarantee, thou will admit dealing with the devil, for I can smell him on thy breath; it reeks of evil.'

She gagged, tasting the bitterness of bile, as a warm, frothing glob of saliva hit her mouth, soiling her lips with his ale-soaked breath.

'Thou shall hang. I shall see to it personally. I will have this village rid of the like of thee and thy kin. Witches.'

One last tug, a matted knot of hair ripped from her scalp, it hung, a knitted mass betwixt his fingers. Awash with blood, it dripped. A cry left her mouth in a pitiful squeal, 'twas as much as she could muster.

She crumpled to a heap on the floor.

Chapter Two

'Fly away home, little sparrow…'

The light through the tiny window was brighter now, yet her bearings were lost. Disorientated, befuddled. Unsure how much time had passed, the maiden sat, hunched, her back pressed to the solid wall.

Squinting at the light, bringing a hand up to her face, she flinched at the pain. She felt her nose, broken, split, her cheeks swollen, bruised. Her skin was no longer wet, but scabbed lumps of clotted, congealed blood clung.

Closing her eyes again, she drifted, sleep taking her mind, a dazing, blurring, a muddle of bewilderment. She longed to be home. Mother would be baking, could almost smell it, taste it upon her tongue. Her sister, sitting, her daughter betwixt her knees, brushing her long dark locks. Oh, her dear, beloved, little Sarah.

Thud, the door swung open. The woman, the old one, limped into the room.

'Stand up. Stand up, girl.'

She tugged at her arms, pulling her up, her back scuffing the harsh stonewall; she felt a drop of blood trickle down her shoulder blades.

'I said, stand up.' The woman dragged her to the middle of the room. 'There,' she pushed. 'Do not move.'

The woman left, as tersely as she had arrived. For a moment, the girl hoped, wondered. The door ajar creaked on its hinges; a draught gushed through the room. She paused, her mind awhirl with hope.

Could she run? Did she dare?

Slam. Another door. Footsteps, not that of the woman, these were heavy and even. Voices. Two. Male. The man, she recognised his gruff, ale sodden tone. Another, this one, lighter, well-spoken, softer.

Oh. She gasped, swallowing a sour, choking lump. Intently, she listened, straining her ears for an inkling of hope. The voices trailed off, mere wisps on the breeze.

A distant click, a door opened, followed by a soft footfall. Outside, she reasoned. Again, the door squeaked as fresh outside blew its way into her dark, musty hell.

With a belly of fear and heart of hope, the young maiden filled her lungs with faith and sped to the chink. Peering through, the outside winked back, the midday sun danced on the grass. The maiden could smell her freedom, feel justice.

She ran.

Naked and alone. She made for the trees. Grass and soil, cold beneath her soles, she ran with all her might for her life.

Where to go?

Home, that was all she knew. She must make it home. There had been a dreadful injustice, a confusion, a mistake. He would see that. He would make that right. She was innocent.

With no idea of position, direction or where on earth she was, she halted. Bewildered. The coppice was thick, the trees tall, though still winter-worn, their branches bare and sharp with twigs. They gave little cover and no concealment. She needed to continue.

Confused, terrified, she sat. The ground was damp but softer than the stone of that room. There was no doubt she had to move. Make it home.

Voices. Distant, but distinct. Fierce and harried.

She scrambled to her feet, lurching forward, tripping on a gnarled, knotted root. Her head cracked against the tree. Stunned, dazed, she felt a fresh deluge of blood course her forehead.

Feet, dozens of them, behind her, shouts and demands. She felt hopeless, squeezing her eyes tightly shut. A nightmare. This was not real. She could feel her mother and hear her sister's voice. *Get thyself to thy feet, hurry, quickly, thou must make it home.*

She wanted to sleep.

Resigning herself to her fate, her head slipped to the ground, her cheek to the mud, her long, matted hair, a blanket over her battered features. Yes, she would stay awhile; let sleep take her. Perhaps the reaper would pity her doomed soul, take her now, rather than leaving her to the mercy of those consumed by hate.

Get up. Quickly.

A hand grabbed hers, pulling, hauling the maiden to her feet. With dazed eyes, a blur of stark, skeletal trunks flashed her vision. Whacks, blows to her body, face, as they thrashed and beat. Betwixt the trees, she ran. Her mind, unable to dodge the dense coppice, the trees victorious in the battle.

Eventually, dragged into the clearing, the wood behind, her hazy vision grasped its bearings.

She looked down at her hand, empty; she was alone. The field yonder, she was almost home. She could see the chimney smoke weaving its enticement above the thatch. If she could just make it to the lane, she would see home. Mother would be there, waiting for her; she would make all right with the world.

Damp beneath the raw soles of her feet. Long, green blades lapped and lashed at her naked legs. With no regard to the increasingly loud yelling in her wake, she coursed on. Home, the thought of her kin compelling her forward.

The lush meadow underfoot gave way to the ditch. Its sheer drop, a sludge of thick mud. It took her. The fall, coating her thin nakedness with cold, sticky sludge. She lay, sprawled at the bottom, amid the broken twigs, the mulch of undergrowth and festering remains of vermin and pests.

Get up. Get up and run.

The voice called from inside her skull. But she could not move. Running a hand over her body, she swiped away the dirt, the sodden muck of old life.

A hand reached down, grabbed her arm, yanking her up, her feet scrambling to gather balance.

Get up, now, child.

Digging her toes and fingertips into the deep mud, she heaved. Her knees pushing hard, she climbed. Grasping, clutching at old tree roots, she pulled her body out. Slumped on the verge, she breathed the grass, the scent of early spring in her nose.

A great sigh filled her soul, her tired eyes closed, her thoughts fading – maybe, if I just lay here, sleep awhile? A slight touch to her face, a gentle voice whispered.

Run home.

It took her hand, pulling, she held on tightly, strong fingers folding around her hand. Warmth spread through her arm, sparking a wave of great intent, jolting her heart with a great firebolt. She would make it home.

Run, run, run. Once more, the voice loud betwixt her ears, thundering sparks of light behind her eyes. *Run for home.*

Soft, almost in flight. The scent of sun-kissed grass caressed her senses as her toes skimmed the tops of the blades. Feather-light rays of the afternoon sun skipped across her naked skin, glistening, glowing with youth and beauty. Birds chirped above her head, swooping, escorting her home, coursing her journey.

As if in her own flight, the maiden spread her arms, stretching her fine, withering limbs, as her fingers teased the dancing breeze. Her face to the warm sun glow, she breathed in life.

Swift, harsh, crack. Her head abruptly met the solid trunk of the great oak. She thundered to the ground; her body crunched beneath its boughs.

This tree spoke of home. It spoke of truth, of love, untainted by these atrocious accusations of witchcraft.

This tree had stood, steadfast and true, for generations, watching, standing guard over her kith and kin.

Huge boughs, ripely laden with seasons gifts, greens and golds. Even in its skeletal poise, it marked its position as majestic custodian, where she had sat as a child, beneath its protection, observing.

Watching him. Watching her.

Thundering pain shot through her skull, her hands clutching her face, tearing away the agony, blood, a new crimson river devouring her face.

The darkness was coming, creeping ever deeper, clawing its inky talons into the soft flesh of hope. Only dark despair was left, the light, and all that be good, 'twas swallowed whole.

At this moment, the maiden's heart and will, shattered. Crushed beneath the heavy foot of superstition.

Chapter Three

'Thou can break my bones...'

The sentinel dissolved. The great oak's immense lumbering weight of its boughs, no more than a wisp, encircling her hope. Leaving her broken belief, once again in the stark reality of her prison.

How evil her mind to play such cruel deceits.

Foolish girl.

The young maiden's fingertips reached to grasp the last threads of home, of her kin. The cavernous pit of loneliness becoming real as it gnawed at her guts. Bitter bile reaping its way to her gullet, vomiting, her last drop of truth and justice. A dark void now devoured her soul.

A shadow grew over her bare skin, dampening the afternoon light. Her naturally fragile frame sat hunched as her willowy limbs clutched her knees tightly to her bust. The dull beat, a sound she now hardly recognised, dimly drummed in her chest, crept its way to her skull.

She ached.

'Get up.'

She could not move, fatigued, her eyes closed, lost faith had stolen all power for the task. Even concentration had abandoned her.

No. She resigned herself to remain. Hunched in the corner of this stone gaol, and die.

'I said, get up.'

The figure kicked. She could hear the swish of skirts, the muffled footsteps, the dragging of a foot. It was the woman.

She could hear her limp, smell her hatred, almost taste her fear. Why did she fear?

Scraping wood on stone, the woman placed the chair in the middle of the room once again. The maiden could hear sighs, huffing, 'twas all she could do to open an eye, her face swollen, sore, broken. The old woman stood behind the chair, her eyes closed, gripping the top. A gentle shard of afternoon sun striking her hands. They were gnarled, twisted, worn. Pain painted the woman's features, and the girl stared.

Her instincts were to comfort, soothe her suffering; she knew of some things, things she had learnt from her mother, watching and listening, not all she understood, but she had learnt, keenly.

'Are thou in pain?' her words felt minuscule as they left her lips. They slipped without thought, merely compassion.

Astonished, wide-eyed, the woman cowered a little. Taking her hands and wrapping them in her skirts. She considered the girl for a moment.

'Please, I mean no . . .'

The words were left unsaid. What did she mean? No harm? Of course, she meant no harm, but as that innocent sentiment began to fall from her lips, stark reality dawned. They feared her. That is why she is here. Hateful words, spiteful shouts, she had suffered them all, yet this was not the same. They were not thoughts of *foolish, simple girl* that seeped from their actions; these were of hatred and fear.

The woman, before her, beneath her fury and haste to rip the cloth from her skin, was indeed in fear. Her poor brain was still trying to gather the threads of reasoning. So confused.

'Do not speak. I will not hear thy fearful scorn and malicious intent to harm.'

'Please, why am I here. I am innocent.'

'That is what they all say.'

'I want to go home; I want my mother.'

'Quiet.'

With that, the woman limped, with hurried steps, to the door. It slammed on her departure.

She was alone again. She stared at the chair; it mocked her.

†

Course rope twisted and bound. The mocking chair was now her custodian, taunting ever louder.

The young maiden was seated. Naked in humiliation, her young womanhood, her virtue, exposed, disgraced and sullied with shame.

She sat upon the worn seat, crossed legged, her knees pushing down on her ankles. Her hands knotted in the small of her back, shoulders bound to the top of the chair, her back unnaturally, excruciatingly, arched, with her breasts shoved forward, exposed and painfully scored with binding.

She was trussed. The thick rope tight, bleeding into her skin. Agony had already settled, marking its territory.

Rumours, stories of the horrific methods, had seeped into the ears of the townsfolk, dripping with moral worth—the work of the witchfinders.

Had it been innocence, pure naïve character, her soft temperament, that had protected her from this horror, merely to be what had delivered her to this moral torture?

His dark face appeared, shadowing her. Stale ale, familiar to her senses. She opened her eyes to find his watching; a tinge of something glistened within.

'Are thou ready?' Circling the chair, sweeping his hands across her skin, they halted on her breasts. He gripped her nipple, twisting it in his fingers; she felt the glee in his touch. 'Confess.'

That word again. It rung in her ears.

'Are thou so naïve to consider that there be a choice?'

The maiden sealed her lips tight. She had no words to give. No words of confession. Of the devil's work. She was no more a witch than he. She merely shook her head, gritting her teeth, a shield against the growing pain.

'So be it.' He turned, facing the woman on his departure. 'Watch her. But take heed, do not speak to her. Do not be fooled by this fool. The devil himself speaks through her simple lips.'

The maiden could see the woman cower and shrivel.

†

They had left her bound, seated upon the chair, watched, for the rest of that day. Dusk had fallen with the fading sun, and the moon had risen in its wake to fill the gaping hole left in the soulless sky. A candle, a single bare flame, lit the cold space—the old woman custodian of the meagre light.

As a new day crept into the room, the others arrived to join the old woman. They had brought a box. No words had been uttered to the maiden; she had simply been pricked. He had watched.

Silver instruments, darning needles, sharp pins, held firmly within the grasp of those God-fearing women. Skilfully, they had stabbed, lightly at first, then with more eager intent, but, all the while, careful in their execution, scarcely a drop of blood had trickled from her wounds, tiny punctures of flesh. Oh, the pain had been immense. Taking the breath from her lungs, stunning her into shock, she had sat motionless, the bonds of her mocking custodian still tight.

Finally, and again, with no word to her, they had unbound her. For a moment, she had just stared at them. She did not move. She could not. Her limbs had fused, her legs bound in a crossed twist, had seized, her muscles in perpetual spasm. The pain so great, she had become numb.

The old woman reached behind, unbound her hands, bringing her arms forward. She had heard her joints creak and pop inside her skeleton, the clicking ricocheting through her body. She looked down at her hands as unknown objects in her lap, they belonged to another, they had no feeling, no blood. They lay limp.

With her body rigid, fixed in its contortion, she had been dragged to the floor. Heaved to stand, her legs failing, twisting, diminishing her to a whimpering heap. For the merest of moments, she had been allowed to stay, sobbing in her private misery. One of them, younger, no more than her own years, had reached down, held out her hand. Slowly, she had been allowed to stand; in her own time, she had gathered her limbs, somehow made them behave as hers. Though, as the maiden gazed down at her naked, bruised, abused body, it belonged to another. She no longer recognised it.

'Walk.'

The words disturbed her wandering, her mind halting on the brink of escape. The voice tethered her existence back to her present hell.

'Walk.'

He stood by the door, hand resting on the handle, as he looked at her. She could not help but muse over his tired expression as her poor mind deliberated over the instructions, with no comprehension of their meaning. Agony highlighted her beaten features.

'Thou are to walk.' He pointed to the far wall, 'to there, back and forth.'

'Come.' The old woman stepped forward, clutching the maiden by her elbow, gently pulling her. She watched her feet as she timidly placed one in front of the other. With each step, a blast of pain shot from her soles, through her legs, snaking through her spine, exploding in a tide of tears, 'til the pain died and eased. The next step brought another wave of agony.

Upon reaching the far wall, the maiden pressed her head against the stone. Pushing her forehead, as if hoping to be devoured by it, become one with the stone, and escape her hell.

'Again!' He spat. 'Thou shall walk 'til thy feet bleed, or thou shall speak the truth.' With that, he left.

She had no recollection of time nor her own state. No thoughts consumed her mind. She was blackness itself. She had been instructed to walk; she had done so, with no option than to concede to his demands. She had no truth to give them; indeed, none they wanted to hear. She had muttered the word innocent, beneath her breath, betwixt the sobs and snuffle of tears, as her feet indeed bled upon the cold, stone floor.

†

With blood-stained feet festering with torn blisters and dirt, she had remained where she had fallen.

Now, for three suns and three moons, she had floundered in her own vomit and waste. Deprived of food. Starved of sleep. They had poked, shouted, shook her to a state of not consciousness, oblivion.

Her mind was neither awake nor asleep. Her eyes could neither see nor were blind. She was in limbo—a frightful place of purgatory.

Waiting.

After her torment and torture, whilst at her lowest, they had questioned. Commanded her, demanded answers and her submission.

An unrelenting battering of allegations and accusations. She had tried to dispute. Lay grievance to their claims. Alas, her plight had fallen mute to their readiness to comply with his wishes. She had heard her own voice deny them, but, as she now lay, a mass of knotted nerves, even she doubted the verdict of her petition.

The Devil's Whore. Witch.

Once more, her body retched as the vicious tang of bile scorched her throat. She tried to move. She could not—her limbs, heavy as lead, her bones, numb beneath her thin shroud of skin.

There, it rose once more, the sun. It crept the wall, peering through the small window above her head. She traced the line of the beam with weary eyes as it hit the filthy, stone floor. She attempted to straighten her leg, to let it rest in the beam of light. To warm her bones.

Dust motes flickered and danced, enticing her into their frolics. Allowing them to take her on their merry dance, she closed her eyes; she wandered on long, warm recollections— carefree days of younger years, of childhood, of kith and kin.

Chapter Four

'Take heed, blame will lead to ruin…'

The fire roared, warming the cottage, floor to rafter.

The crone stood beside the pot, stirring continuously but with no conscious attention. Her old eyes watched the bubbles swell and burst, though her mind was elsewhere. The harsh stab of guilt rushed with each boiling eruption, never bursting, instead bloating, suffocating her.

Framed by the door aperture, hands clutching her silver amulet, her daughter watched. She could sense the pain, share the panic, the dread. But the guilt was solely hers. It was burrowing these past few days, digging deep inside her ribcage.

'Mother.'

The crone was lost in the depths of her private thoughts. Her mind had drifted to warmer, brighter days.

'Mother.' Her skirts skimmed the floorboards, her steps soft and silent. Her hand rested on the old crone's shoulder. 'Please, Mother, I am fearfully sorry. But thou does see, I had no choice. . .' the words drifted.

Those words, the plea, the sentiment, it was the same that had been cast for the past three suns and moons. Those words no longer held their meaning.

Neither had slept, a few snatched moments, where sleep had dragged them under, only to drown them in horrors they could barely imagine.

'Mother, I beg of thee . . . thou must speak to me.'

With a gentle nudge, the crone shrugged her daughter's hand away. A long sigh left her old body. Turning to face her, for the first time in days, she beheld her daughter's eyes. What was it that darkened her eyes, fear, dread, loss or hatred?

'The fault of which we now suffer, of which thy poor sister suffers, it should be for thou to keep. I wonder on her sanity, her poor heart, so naïve, so simple.' She sat heavily upon the stool, the fire glow reflecting in her eyes, as she bothered the flames with the iron poker. 'Yet, we must stay strong. Blame: it can play no part; no good can come from it. It will consume thy heart 'til no love remains.'

'The blame will always be mine to carry.'

'Be careful, daughter. I see the darkness within. Be careful it does not devour the light.'

'I would never . . .' She stopped, considering the next few words. To express what was in her heart, what thoughts had taken root in the pit of her belly, this would be sure to evoke her mother's suspicions. Yet, as she stood, gazing into her mother's eyes, she knew all too well the darkness that was leaching from her own. She had felt the glances; mother had seen them, those tiny flashes of something, what, she was unable to say. She was not sure it had a name, but it was taking root.

'Be sure not to. For I fear they will come knocking, and this time their claims may hold the truth they are so ready to cling to.'

'They do it in his name. If I had meddled, stopped—'

'No more.' The crone's hand rose, poker still gripped tightly betwixt her swollen knuckles. 'My poor heart can hear no more.'

'Once the sun is high, I shall go into the village, inquire. See if there be any gossip. Any news? We must hear soon;

there has been no word. No trial, surely, we can see her. There has been no . . .'

'No, do not say it.'

'But, if there has been no . . .' she faltered a moment, the word stuck in her throat. Taking a deep breath, 'there has been no hanging.'

The word solidified, falling, plummeting to the floor, destroying all hope they still clung to.

'Do not attempt to undo what has been done. Thou made a choice, now thou must, we all must, stand by and watch.' The crone sighed; her chest crackled as she coughed to clear it. 'Thy dearest sister has gone; they took her, they did not take thee.' She stared, shocked by her own spite. 'If thou continue to meddle, asking, they shall surely come again. And all will be undone. She would have been sacrificed . . . for nothing. It would have been for nothing.'

Tears prickled the crone's eyes. They were weak, weary.

Holding her mother's gaze, watching the iron poker as she lowered it to the grate once more. She wondered about her stability. She pained at her new vulnerability; her strength had been fading of late, she slept very little, she ate even less. If she lost her mother, she would be alone, but for her child.

'Mother, thou should eat. Surely, it is cooked now. Go sit.'

Her heavy paces took her to the chair; it sat, nestled betwixt the fireplace and window. She could see the great oak through the leaded panes. It stood, gazing back at her.

'Those were happy times. My daughters playing. Smiles, laughter, love. Those are the days that take my thoughts; all too often, I forget the now, the hatred and fear that grips us. Oh, to hear laughter once more.' Her head rested against the dark wood. 'He was not always so powered by his hatred.'

Silently, the woman ladled the thick broth into a bowl. There were no words to aid this moment, to mollify, reconcile the moment, or add to her mother's reminiscent wanderings. Delving into the past led only to a sorry path, of once loves and now hates.

It would only bring forward her darkness.

Handing the bowl to her mother, she left the room. She needed to remove herself from those reminiscent thoughts.

Hovering at the bedroom door, she peered through the chink. The door blew slowly as she watched, holding the frame, pressing her cheek to the wood.

In this breath, all she could see was purity. Her daughter, her dark hair, curled around her chin, her young hands clutching the top of the blanket as it lay nestled beneath her chin. She was pure; she was the purest part of life. If she could hold onto her, keep her close, protect her, it would, in turn, protect her, save her.

Her sister would understand, had they not known that this day may come. For ten years, they had spoken of what would be needed. That protecting the child would be the only importance. Her sister had understood; she had seen herself in the girl, after all.

As she watched the sleeping child, she knew, in her heart, that no matter what, her sister would save Sarah, just as she had done.

Chapter Five

'Does healing light spark from thy fingertips?'

Mud clung to her soles, the soft leather, supple with moisture, the lane damp with early spring.

The village was quiet. Perhaps they avoided her; maybe there was no word of her sister. Yet, a strangeness crept alongside her as she strode. She felt shadowed by death. Surely, the reaper would allow her enough time to settle the smallest of scores.

She stopped. Dread was beginning to bubble in the pit of her stomach; she wanted to advance, but, around the corner, she knew. She knew that if fate were cruel, and indeed it was, the scaffold would not be vacant. There had been no word of a hanging.

A great inhale of the brisk morning air filled her lungs and heart with a little more hope than before. She rounded the corner. There it was, devoid of any occupants.

She wanted to cry, to weep, pray for thanks, to whoever would listen. Yet, as she stood watching the empty wooden framework, devoid of rope or body, she wondered about her sister, her whereabouts, well-being, and sanity. Surely, someone would have come calling to offer knowledge, even gossip for their own musings.

Even Hopkins himself. Though, would he dare?

†

'There be no word.' She offered her news, but her mother was not listening, vacancy ever more apparent.

Slipping off her shoes, she lay them in the hearth, the fire gently warming the leather, wiping the debris of leaf mulch from the soles, tossing it into the flame. It hissed back at her. She closed her eyes, savouring the warmth, her fingers taut with cold, stretching them in front of the flames.

A knock. It startled, her moment of peace gone. Again, louder, more urgent than the first, another and another.

A boy stood before her, a village youth, his face familiar, his name unknown.

'Please, will thou help? My mother asked for thee.'

'Thy mother. Is she known to me?'

'It's my youngest sister by two, the smallest; she is only five. My mother requests thy help.' He paused, filling his lungs, before the words again spilt in panic. 'She has a fever, has for three nights now. My mother says, if thou cannot help, she will die.'

'Wait there.'

She stepped away from the door, gently pushing it. Paused a moment, wondering of its legitimacy, the honesty of such a plea. No matter. She would go. She could hear the boy sob behind the wood. If it was a ploy, then so be it.

Her mother motioned with a hand. 'Go. If it is true, then the child needs help.'

†

The boy darted along the lane. Her legs barely keeping up, but as she ran, she could hear his heart swamped with fear, panic.

An abrupt halt, his body bent over, hands on his knees, panting. She finally stopped beside him, rubbed his back, as, with a shaking hand, he pointed.

'In there,' he puffed.

The cottage was small, humble, scarcely furnished, though kindly in its warmth. The mother stood by her daughter's bedside, her face painted with an expression every mother could feel, anguish.

The girl child, youngest of five, lay tiny, frail in the centre, her sheets slick, moist with fever. Her skin pale, translucent; sweat beaded her brow and chapped her lips. Life was hanging by a single thread, gently tethered to her mother.

She had seen it before, could help, but, oh, the cost would be high. Closing her eyes, gathering her thoughts, her compassion for life and the sight of her sleeping daughter resolved her heart over any notion of her safety.

'The fever, I have seen it before.'

'Can thou help?' the mother wept on her knees, clutching the woman's skirt in a plea.

'Please, we have very little, but, whatever the costs, we shall pay,' gulping down her tears, paused, stared straight at the woman. 'I have heard thou can help when others can no longer. I have tried everything. She is my child, my blood.'

'I can . . .' hesitating a moment, she saw her daughter lying before her.

'Please, my daughter . . .'

'There be no cost. If I can help, I shall. All I ask is for thou to keep thy dealing silent.'

Taking her hands, holding them tight, her eyes wandered the room; indeed, there was little of value. The mother's eyes narrowed for a breath, fear gripped.

'What is it thou mean to do to my child?'

'No . . .' squeezing her hands, 'all I asked is for discretion.' Softening her tone, she sighed, 'Some of the townsfolk would mark my family as . . . other than Godly. This is not true. We are but healers. That is why thou called for me. It is a remedy.'

Meaning, understanding, embarrassment covered the mother's sorrowful features. She stood, placing a hand on the woman's cheek, and smiled.

'Thy sister,' she nodded solemnly. 'I have heard they keep her still.

'My sister? What is it thou knows?'

'Thy sister is said to be a witch, but she claims innocence. It is said that she be alive. They are keeping her for him.'

That one word, a single utterance of *him,* could bring the sky in around her, sinking her heart into darkness. Gathering herself, she headed for the door.

'Please, my daughter?'

'I shall return this evening,' and closed the door behind her.

†

Dusk had fallen in ritual, while, this night, so heavy, as if the Goddess moon herself, had swept a great heavy curtain across the fields. Its closeness thrust down around her shoulders, prickling her skin, as she left the cottage. Her mother stood watch at the door as she headed into the lane. Although her own daughter was safely inside the walls of home, a growing fear began to fester inside her gut.

There had been no uttered words of her sister or what news she had received, her lips tightly knitted together, keeping those words within. The crone was in no fit state to tolerate them. The mere mention of *him* would have brought a new wave of melancholy to pile amidst the ever-growing angst of her sister's wellbeing. Instead, her efforts were focused on concocting the remedy for that poor child. She had seen her own staring back at her, the mother's pain gushing tangibly through her own veins.

The humble home insight, she rounded the corner, holding her breath, her back to the wall, before advancing further—an ever-increasing sense of calamity hammered in her breast.

At the front door, already ajar, she was greeted by the son who had fetched her—a small fire in the grate, the girl's mother pacing the bare floorboards.

'Thou came?'

'I said I would return.'

'Please, this be my mother.'

An old woman sat beside her grandchild, aged, gnarled, fingers gently teased blonde strands of hair from the young girl's brow. The old woman made no attempt to move or acknowledge her until she approached and sat beside the girl. She took the child's hand, holding her fingers around her wrist; there was a rash, an irritation, a pink bloom to her tender skin.

'She is very weak. Thou must pray and have faith.' She glanced at the cross around the old woman's neck, her hand seeking out her silver amulet.

'Can thou save the child?' The old woman stared deep into her eyes, pain evident in every line and crease.

'Yes.'

'Then quickly, then thou must go, leave.'

'I am only here to save the child, not by my wish.'

'Nor mine.' Her words were spat, although beneath the harsh old façade was a separate, private pain.

'I mean no harm.'

'Then get on with it, and leave.'

The bottle was small, removing the cork, holding it fast; she eased the child's head from the pillow to take the mixture. Her lips parted, barely conscious, taken by sleep and fever. Her eyes fluttered as she swallowed the concoction.

'Let her rest. Watch and pray. I can return in the morning, before first light to . . .'

'No.' The old woman glared. 'No, for your sake, do not return. If thou has not saved the child this night, then thou will not be able to save her another.'

Her words were solid, with a truth that even she could not deny. Still, she could not help but feel a threat lay within the weave of that response.

Gathering her bag, she wrapped her shawl about her shoulders and smiled at the girl child, tenderly placed a hand upon her brow, silently praying for her delicate soul.

With her hand on the doorknob, the mother thanked and wept. That pain, it could so easily be her own; she understood that undeniable bond. Her own eyes tingling, standing on the threshold, the night bleeding in, wrapping its inky arms.

'Thy sister?'

Taken aback by the words, she stumbled out into the dark, gripping the doorframe with white fingertips. The old woman stood, in the doorway, eyes softened by the candle she held.

'What of my sister? What does thou know? Please, I beg if thou has word, please share it.'

'She is still alive. I know not of their plans. There has been no word of hanging or ducking.'

'Where is she . . . I need?'

'They will not allow it. For pity's sake, thou must forget her. She is lost; she will be gone soon.'

Stepping over the threshold, her leg trailing behind, the old woman dithered into the night. She paused, watching the flame dance in the night breeze. Gripping the candlestick tighter, pushed it further into the darkness. It glowed betwixt them, both faces distorted by dancing shadows.

'I have seen what thou have done here this night.'

'We are but healers. We do not deal with the devil.' She laughed; despite the seriousness and pain that drenched her heart, she could not help but laugh.

'There be others who do not share those thoughts.'

'And what of thy thoughts?'

The old woman paused, watching the shadows play on the woman's features.

'Thou came to save the child; what thou have done is yet to be seen. But no. I do not think thy kin to be witches. I have not seen the devil at work this night.'

'And of Hopkins, what of him?' Her heart hated the name; she felt its poison ooze onto her tongue.

'I have not seen him. They say she is known to him. They say . . .' she drifted off. 'I have said too much.'

The old woman grabbed her hand, almost inspecting the woman's fingers. She turned it over in hers and stared up into her face.

'She will be dead soon, one way or another. They shall not suffer her to live. I have witnessed it before. I have seen it in their eyes. Even though I have seen no evil in hers and none in here this night.'

With no more words or gestures, the old woman turned and limped back inside the cottage. The door slammed behind her.

Chapter Six

'If thou will not save thyself…'

A bang. Loud, it harshly awoke the maiden from her memories.

The door swung back from the wall as it hit it hard, then eagerly flung shut. She tried to look up at the figure. Her head ached on her shoulders; her neck was stiff. Only her eyes moved in her otherwise motionless husk of a body.

He simply stared.

There was an air of disbelief about his features, a gaze of scepticism, of misgiving.

No words were uttered from his lips. Instead, he removed his hat, holding it to his chest, almost an act of sympathy, of condolence. Her heart leapt. For a breath, she hoped for compassion. She looked directly up at his face. His eyes wore a wide stare, held fast on hers. Upon opening her mouth to speak, his hand raised to halt her words. He lowered, crouching next to her thin body. The broadness of his shoulders blocked the sun rays, and the dust motes vanished with the folly of her thoughts.

Running his fingers along her arm, his head tilted, his eyes closed as if voyaging his own melody of long ago.

He sighed.

She gasped as his hand went to her breast. Her body transfixed, sat at his mercy as he explored and caressed her skin. His fingers about her, squeezing. His eyes on hers. She wanted to scream.

He dragged his hand down her body. She gawped, wide-eyed, as his fingers slid between her legs. Harsh and needy, he pushed, taking and grabbing her womanhood. The shame brought a wave of sickness over her soul. Her eyes, huge and fearful, pleaded with his.

Blinking, he swiftly removed his hand. They both looked at it with fear and contempt. She wanted to touch, to take it in hers. To find some gentleness amongst all this cruelty. As she moved, he snatched her wrist. Gripping it tightly.

'No.' He glowered at her.

He rubbed his thumb across her parchment skin. She could see it; his eyes were brimming with those long-buried memories, which swept in on daydreams. He swallowed. He almost spoke; she could feel the words, but she did not hear them. They both watched her hand glisten as his tightened around her wrist. It whitened, the blood draining from her veins.

He smiled, leaning into her.

'Thou will tell. Give me what I want. Thou will tell me what I want to hear.' His words lingered at her ear as his breath sighed warmth to her cheek. 'I promise thee that.'

'Matthew.'

'This can all be over.'

'I beg of thee.'

'There be no room left for begging. Thou simply must tell. The whole town knows what thou are.'

'Matthew, please?'

'Thou have no right, no position to be so familiar.' Her wrist slipped from his grasp. His fingers released, but they lingered in hesitation as her skin teased his. He quietly stood, turned his back on the girl.

'Please, Matthew. What great wrong have I done to deserve this, for, in thy heart, thou know it to be so?'

'No more. Just give me what I want.'

'Thou knows this be wrong, Matthew, please help me?'

'Thou shall pay for thy wrongdoings.' A great audible sigh left his chest in a persistent crackle. He wheezed. He coughed. He spluttered.

She wanted to console him, to ease him. Mother had taught her how to heal; she had watched and noted as her sister worked. She could help him, but she did not move.

'Is there no goodness left in thy heart, Matthew? No compassion. No, remembrance?'

'Remembrance?' he spat bitterly. 'It is for the remembrance which I ask thee to tell me, for we all know what dwells beneath that pretty skin.' Gliding his fingers over her thigh, he winced, recoiling his hand. 'There was once beauty, and truth, and purity.'

'Matthew, I beg of thee, no more.'

'I remember all. Does thou remember?

'I do not understand. Why am I here?'

'Give me a name.' He paused, watching her face.

'My sister?'

'Name her. I want her.'

'Thou knows my sister. I do not understand.'

'Thy sister!'

'What? What, Matthew, what are thou asking?'

'Name her as a witch, and I shall be lenient.'

'NO!'

He snatched at her wrist once more, gripping hard into her smooth skin. He could not help but watch as his fingers drained the life from it. He watched, and he waited.

'Please, Matthew. I beseech thee, let go, thou are hurting me.'

'Come now. Name thy sister, and I shall stop this. I shall spare thee.'

'Spare me? I am innocent. Innocent of what thou deem to be so. I am not, and thee knows me. How can I give thee mine own sister? My kin, I will not cast out my sister to save my own life.'

'So, thou would rather hang than name her. After all that passed?'

Easing his grip, he brushed the hair from her face, smoothing the wild mess down about her shoulders. He ran his fingers through her dark locks, teasing a long strand; he curled it around his finger.

'Thou knows, I have thee at my mercy. This town listens to my word. If I deem thee to be innocent, they shall listen and heed my wishes. But . . .'

'But?'

He twisted the strand tighter, pulling at her scalp, pulling her face to his. His eyes intent, his nose touching hers. He brushed his lips against hers. They lingered there, and his tongue licked. He pushed his mouth hard, taking what he wanted. She allowed his advances. Static, she could not move. She had no desire to move. Slowly, he released. His eyes closed; she watched his face. A great whirling swirl of confusion swam through her body. He looked at her.

'But . . . if I announce thee to be a witch, thou shall hang this day. Before the sun falls once more, thou shall be no more than a memory.'

'I will not. How can I name mine own sister, announce her to be a witch?'

'Because, if thou does not, then thou shall die.' He stood, looking down at her. 'Thou knows what she is.'

'She is my own blood, my kin.'

'Thou have heard the claims. Thou have heard the gossip. Thou know more so than anyone that they are true, that she be the Devil's Whore.'

The girl staggered to her feet, her legs barely able to hold her upright. His stare boring holes into her heart.

'This be wrong, so very wrong, Matthew. She is not a witch. I am not a witch; I am wrongly accused. Thou knows this to be the truth. Despite what has passed betwixt us, that thou would send me to the noose. Does thee not love me? I love thee.'

Her legs gave way as she crumpled to the stone floor, her batted nakedness, her bare feet ridden with dirt and muck, as the coldness burrowed into her bones.

For a second, he faltered. He pulled her to her feet. Her back pushed hard and heavy against the stone wall, her eyes looked up into his.

'My heart would, it be true, pain at the sight of thou hanging from the noose, for those memories. Therefore, I ask thee once more. Name thy sister so I may release thee from this.' He rubbed his finger down her cheek, thumb across her lips, across the curve of her chin, down to her neck. 'All this may end this day if thou would just name thy sister. I shall have them release thee.'

Closing her eyes, she shook her head. 'No.'

'This be the only chance to save thyself. This town shall have a hanging; they want blood.'

'Then may it be so. May I swing from that noose this day before the sun falls? May I never see another night, and never new dawn rise above my roof. I am disgraced by thy words, Matthew; think of my poor mother.'

'And what of my mother?'

'I understand not. Thy mother?'

She stared, adamantly, with defiance, then a twinge, just a tiny spark at first, it began to ignite, blazing her vision. Her thoughts went to that day, that night of day. She was confused; her naïve mind battled memories of screams, weeping and blood. But, no matter how she desperately tried to unravel them, the images mingled into a great whirling mix of shadows and faces. Horrid, terrified faces screamed at her.

She clenched her eyes tight, shaking her head to rid them from her thoughts. Upon opening them, he stared at her, daggers for eyes that hurt her poor heart.

'I remember thy mother, Matthew.'

He clutched her throat. 'I will have her and what she keeps from me.' He swallowed a torturous lump. 'Maybe I should hang thee from thy ankles.'

His fingers tightened around her windpipe as his eyes traced the thinness of her body, the meagreness of her once ample breasts.

He ran his tongue over his lips. He opened his mouth to speak, but the words lay heavy, burdened on his tongue.

Her eyes widened. Her face reddened as she gripped his fingers. Frantically, she struggled. Her whisper-thin arms flailing, lashing at his chest. In a pathetic attempt to remove his hands, her nails dug hard into his flesh. Her legs scrambled to keep her footing, but she hung from his grip, her legs useless. Her muffled screams bellowed in her skull but, without breath, remained mute. She was drifting. She could see those memories once more—soft dreamy days.

He squeezed tighter.

Her face paled. Her eyelids fluttered. He could feel her failing, slipping down the wall, her feet hopeless beneath her weight. He let go. Leaving her to fall, to collapse into a heap. Hitting the stone-hard, her head smashed against the wall, spattering thick blood, decorating his boots.

He gazed down at the body on the floor and strode to the door. His hand faltered, just for a moment. His fingers reached for the handle, then recoiled, making a fist. He looked back over his shoulder. His words fell to the ground.

'I release thee, in hope, that it may release me also.'

Chapter Seven

'As old wounds ooze fresh blood, new sparks ignite.'

Whack. She hammered, banged, flogged with her bare hands, kicked, hollered. She would gain access one way or another. If they did not open the door, she would rip it from its hinges or take it apart, nail by nail, plank by plank.

Blood smeared the ends of her digits, yet she wavered not. Her heart was blackened by their hatred. Her kin, they had taken, tortured, murdered. All she now desired was her sister's body. And, if they did not allow her this, after the destruction they had caused, then so be it. Destruction of her own making would befall them, around the ears of those misguided do-gooders, who wreak havoc upon innocent lives in the name of God.

Now, high above the tiles, the sun beamed. Cursing its hope, she stopped.

He was there, inside. All she had asked was to see her sister.

She kicked the door, her toe throbbed, she kicked it again. Her pain, nothing compared to that of her sister's. Her heart plummeted as she collapsed to her knees, sat where she fell.

For two suns and moons, she had seen nothing, but the cursed vision of her sister's body, batted, torn, bruised, dead. However, these were mere speculations her own tortured mind had conjured. She could not fathom the reality that may await her on the other side of this door. She thumped the wood, her fist split as a scarlet drop stained her lap.

Clunk. A metal lock, a bolt dragged, its clanking echoed through the building.

Standing, she staggered back, taking a pace down the step. Like thunder betwixt her ears, the pounding of her heart deafened as blood rushed. Her face burned.

With creaking hinges, the great door gave way to a figure; he strode forward, resting on the threshold.

'I want my sister.'

She had no time; the moment for pleasantness long passed. Only the intent to retrieve what belonged to her and placed within the sanctuary of home.

'Thy sister is dead.'

'I want my sister. I need to take her home. Surely, thou cannot deny me that?'

A stilted expression on his face, he stepped forward, down the step—his face level with hers.

'It has been many years.'

'How?'

'What? How, what?'

'How did thou murder her?'

'Come now.'

'Matthew, my sister is dead. I request the knowledge of how this came to be. Thou had her taken, dragged, all in the name of God. Named her witch, but there has been no trial, no execution. Yet, she is dead. So, I ask again, how did thou murder her.'

'Thy sister . . .' he paused, taking his hat from his head, holding it to his chest. 'She would not give me what I wanted. She would not save herself.' His head bowed.

'Thou walk in the glory of God, speaking of good and pure thoughts. Do these folk who employ thee and thy services, do they know the great pretence with which thou walk?'

'I am not scared of thee, witch.'

'Thou calls me a witch?' she stepped back, the mere closeness of him stinging her skin. 'I am not a witch, nor was my sister. Thou cast these accusations with hate that I can now see dominates thy soul. Matthew, has thou forgot love?'

Reaching forward, he took her elbow, his hand grazing past breasts that heaved beneath her corset. Gently, with a smile, he guided her along. She followed. Stepping over the threshold into the dark, her eyes desperate to adjust from the midday sun.

'Come.'

Continuing to guide her, opening a door, he led her inside to a simple room, a table, two chairs and a shelf with books, ledgers.

'Matthew, thou has come far, a simple law office to this.' Her smirk did not go unnoticed, but he chose to ignore it.

'Sit. Please. Let us be of civil tongue this day. Thou have come for thy sister, and thy sister I shall give. But, first, let us talk.'

Taking his seat, he looked at her across his makeshift desk, gesturing to the vacant chair. Reluctantly, she sat down, hard.

'What is it thou wants from me?' She spat. Those words came at a price; she already knew what he desired. She had done everything to suppress this moment, to a mere maybe.

'Would thou care for a drink?'

'I would rather choke.'

'That, I could soon arrange,' he grinned.

'I have no desire to play games.'

'Ah, but I am deadly serious.'

Swallowing hard, she coolly examined her bloody hands. 'I am not here to talk. All I want is to take my poor sister home.'

'Well, now that is such a shame. Has it not been many years since we last spoke?'

'My sister, Matthew.'

'We shall, no doubt, come to the matter of thy sister. But first, please, indulge me.'

Reclining, his shoulders relaxed, his hands folded in his lap, she could see the boy that once was, smiling back at her. He had always been of a beauty that would turn heads, maidens would swoon and pander. She, herself, had mused how golden sparks seeped from his skin as if the Goddess moon herself had granted it so. The memory fired steel bolts through her heart, pinning her to the chair, in the here and now. She burned with hatred. Yet, beneath the sting of that poison lay another feeling that boiled below the surface, warming her thighs.

'Enough!' standing abruptly, knocking her hip on the table edge. 'Please, I beseech thee. Matthew, I have no desire to rip open old wounds or revel in the pain of long ago.'

'Pain and wounds. I wonder, now, to whom would those belong?' Standing, his arm flung forward, pushing her shoulder 'til she sat once again. 'We are here, together, after all these years. Let us not cast aside this opportunity to mend those wounds. Does thou not owe me at least that?'

The moment swelled betwixt them. His eyes hungrily taking in her body, devouring. She watched, almost amused at his longing, cursed her own.

'Of what I owe thee? Oh, Matthew, has time, these ten long years, muddled those last days in thy memory. 'Twas I that . . .' she stopped.

She had said far too much. To speak of this now would only bring forth more pain. Her heart, as it darkened, could take no more.

'Ah, those last days. I recall those, often,' he signed.

There it was, that light in his eye.

'That beauty still rests upon thy features, Matthew,' her tone tender, wistful. 'Such a pity it does not trickle further into thy heart.'

A smile crept, taking residence on his face, but he replied not.

'I must congratulate thee on such a success; it is spoken of far and wide through the towns and hamlets.' She smiled in return. 'I had heard that thou left to search employ in the realms of law. Admirable, although I see no justice in what thou are doing.'

Pausing, gauging his thoughts, she felt her skin tingle.

'Duty, 'twas my duty to return.'

'Duty?' she shuffled in her seat. 'What of the duty to me, to us?'

His eyes narrowed but remained fixed on her face. His fingers crossed weaved together in his lap. She deliberated as his fingers steepled, pressing the tips together. He brought them up to his lips, patting them in some silent rhythm. A habit that had clearly not left him, a small reminder of the man he once knew. 'Twas clear that he was uncomfortable, nervous. Perhaps, even afraid of her.

His lips parted to speak. 'I have a duty to God.'

'A duty to God?'

'I do not expect thee to understand.'

'How is thy, father?' She added with a smirk.

'Enough of this.' He slammed his hand down onto the wooden surface, a cloud of rising dust particles leapt before her eyes. She blinked as they clung to her lashes.

'I am simply asking after the welfare of thy kin, well, I hope. Alive? Not murdered, by the hands of those thou once loved, called kin.'

He rose, his chair scraping the floorboards until it hit the wall. Fists clenched; he closed his eyes. She gazed in tormented glee; her intention had hit its mark, direct shot betwixt family loyalty and shame.

Dust motes soared from the floorboards; his feet heavily paced the room. She made no more sound, spoke not another word, simply watched him deliberate her words.

He had undoubtedly aged but had she not done the same, they had been mere youths, children themselves. There had been no exchange of words for nigh on ten years, though her heart still felt the sting of that last moment. It had replayed in her head like a theatrical tragedy, reliving it in the dark hours; it had remained both her torment and a place of sanctuary.

Lost in those webbed wanderings, his eyes met hers. His face was close; his warm breath wisped her hair. Perched on the edge of the desk, his fingers glided up her arm, over her shoulder, halting on her breast. She gazed down at his fingers as they swept gently over her skin, now noticing her breathing had increased, her heart now pounded beneath her corset. Her breasts swelled as if to meet his fingertips.

'I have missed the glow of thy skin; it still teases my thoughts. My nights often take on lonely darkness.'

'That darkness, Matthew, comes from within,' she sneered. 'Where light once resided, darkness now sits.'

'Perhaps.'

'Thou left. I was left with more than wistful musings and heated thoughts, Matthew.'

'So, are thou saying, thou have not missed this?' The tips of his fingers teased beneath her corset lacing. 'My eyes see the contrary.'

'I have indeed reflected on my love for thee. My poor heart now bleeds for the love we once shared. I waited for thee. We waited.'

Taking his hand in hers, ceasing it on its quest, she held it tight.

Looking upon them, for a moment, the room disappeared. 'Twas bright dappled sunlight that mottled their skin as they lay beneath the limbs of the great oak. Tones of lush, green foliage. Soft, milky skin freed from the soft, russet of her dress. Her eyes closed, the sun warm, blushing her skin.

'Thou can feel it too; the longing still lives.'

His lips touched hers, his tongue taking her breath, snatching it from her lungs. For a moment, her eyes ablaze with brightness, a glare of clarity, of purity and love.

Then, it was gone.

His tongue caught betwixt her teeth; she gripped it, pressing with the weight of her jaw. That familiar darkness swamped her, smothering the light of goodness, calling forth the unknown name of what she, with all her being, had tried to suppress.

He cried out, the pain sharp, as were her teeth. He pulled away, his fingers caught in her grip, her nails raking scarlet streaks into his skin. He remained pinned. Neither biting further nor retreating, her teeth secured him in the moment along with her penetrating stare.

The swirling black smoke of dark intent, of hatred, of betrayal, of loss and misery swept over her soul, feeding her body the pumping lifeforce of fierce darkness.

In a flash, she released him, both mouth and hands, stood, glaring with eyes of fire. Her vision now emblazoned with tones of black smoke, purple bruised skin, lapped, licked by orange flames. She moved with vision blindness, her feet finding the door. She turned as it cleared, her eyes falling upon the nightmare that played on his features.

'I shall have my sister home; please see that she be returned to me this day. She will rest in peace. She will return to the light after the hell darkness thou saw fit to bestow upon her poor, wretched soul.'

'I am not . . .'

'Do not try me, Matthew. Do not dare to test what thou do not understand.'

'Witch, is it thy true self that shows before me.'

'Do not play with me, Matthew.'

'My name on those plump lips; it teases still.'

With a start, her eyes flashed black, she sprang forward, gripping his chin, his beard betwixt her fingers, she squeezed. Glaring, showing her teeth, a growl rumbled in her chest.

'Thou could not, would not, understand the pain that dwells within my breast, do not begin to judge my motives nor action, when it be thee that scours the countryside, preying on innocent souls as my sister.'

He recoiled, she released as he stepped back to the table; resting there, he rubbed his chin.

'There were claims against her person. She had been named a witch. I . . .'

'She was no more a witch than thee.'

'I am in the employ of this town.' Carefully pacing the floor, he advanced once more, keeping his hesitance low. 'I am to do their bidding; their will is to see the town purified of the devil's dealings.'

'She was not a witch.'

'There was a claim, by a child, then the mother. A claim that strange sounds, dark words of the devil had been heard from thy cottage.'

Her eyes watched his mouth as the words fell, watching for a smirk, a sign of glee, of contentment. None came. Instead, his eyes welled with something other than satisfaction.

'Those claims are false,' she spat. 'Lies.'

'She had been seen. There had been a witness. She had been seen fleeing the cottage by moonlight, naked, bare as the moment she arrived in this world, screaming atop of her lungs, strange words and chants.'

Hidden amongst those words was a truth. An outline of something real, of a curse, a reality that she knew, but not of the devil, nor evil, nor witchcraft.

'She had trusted thee, Matthew. After the closeness of our kith and kin, thou should accept the ramblings of some child to that of thy own heart? For thou know the truth of this. Thou know far too well, the terrible but harmless truth that lies at the heart of this awful accusation. Yet, as thou stand there, as God be thy witness, do not deny me the honesty of thy own heart and acknowledge that my sister was not a witch.'

'And what God be thy witness?'

Taken aback by his statement, she staggered, her heel stubbing the wooden door frame, wedged between the wall and him.

'This is not about me, Matthew.'

'Ah, but it is very much about thee.' Sweeping a stray strand of hair around her ear, his finger trailed down her neck. 'It is all about thee,' he whispered.

'Does torture and torment sit well with thy God, Matthew?'

'My conscience does not weigh heavy. Where I can plainly see thou carry a great weight. It is guilt that sits heavy on thy breast, is it not?'

'No, 'twas not I that dragged a poor, innocent, simple creature from her mother's arms.'

'Thou did not save thy sister.'

'Matthew, thy heart is black,' she hissed, her back leaching into the wall like a cornered fox.

'Thou could have saved her.'

She stared, wide-eyed, through gritted teeth.

'Instead, thou watched as they took her. Remained safe in the cottage, closing the door behind her. Surely, a deed such as that can, and should, weigh greatly indeed. I know that myself, to live with such a dark knowledge, would blacken my soul.'

'Evil. Thy dark heart, Matthew, is there nothing but evil that courses through thy veins? I had no choice. My sister knew.'

'Maybe the devil owns thy soul now?' He replied calmly.

'She knew I could not stop those men; she understood that I had to let them take her.'

'No matter how much those words fall from thy pretty lips, they will never be just, and thou know it to be so. Thou cast thy sister aside to save thy own skin.'

'Not mine, Matthew.'

Studying her face, he watched as her dark eyes swelled wet, puddled. He wiped, smearing a tear across her cheek. Her belly bubbled with revulsion; his fingers lingered far too long on her skin, trailing them down to her throat. She seized his hand. Too strong for him, he pulled away, folding his arms.

'She could have saved herself.' He leant in, glared with blameless eyes as he kissed her cheek.

'As thou would not, I saved thy sister.'

Chapter Eight

'Sadly, she was no longer her Mistress…'

Manningtree - Samhain 1645

Amidst the rotting, decaying afterlife of vermin and mulch, tormented by her own failings, she kept vigil over the cottage, standing her ground and that of her kin. Each night, in waiting, 'til her bones ached with bitter fatigue. Beneath, sheltered by the lumbering boughs of the great oak, her old friend, she sat. Yet, as her eyes lifted to its burnished leaves, she wondered. With all that it had witnessed, she could sense it spurning her, scorning, for both love and hate. It no longer brought comfort to her soul. Rejection fell with those russet leaves of disdain. It had borne witness to deceit, evil, the wrongs of human hearts. Something was coming.

†

With aching joints, the crone staggered to the window. With each movement, she felt her bones ageing, leaning on the ledge, her eyes ever watching. The great oak watched back.

Taking the pewter candlestick, resting it on the ledge, she watched the last of the night's flame. It would soon be spent. Her dear youngest child, she wept for her loss, as she had done each night since. The pain still ever intense.

They had buried her in private, within the confines of their knowledge, by dark and in secret. Her delicate body, broken, disfigured, sullied with bruises, cuts and marks that she could only dare imagine their cause. They had sensitively washed, bathed her body, then carefully wrapped her in cloth, a remnant of home. Then, bound her with love, memories and chants.

Her heart throbbed, cursed him and those others for her daughter's final place of rest. Unhallowed and unmarked. But she is adamant; she must and would rest in peace.

The ground is blessed by her own faith; she had blessed it each day since. Lighting a candle each night to guide her spirit, bring her spirit home. Purgatory is no place to linger.

Now, as the great oak stood this night, she could feel it weep, hear the wind bend its boughs in sorrow. For it now bore witness to the darkness that was swelling. She had seen it coming, perhaps before her daughter.

Dusk had fallen; she had watched, with great sorrow, as her daughter left the cottage, this night as each before. Yet, as each dawn had arisen above the thatch, she had returned ever more distant, more detached, than the one before.

She was blackening, her heart darkening with hatred. However, this night, there had been more than her shadowed heart that darkened her features. Dusk had brought certainty.

She had risen from her stool, with quivering legs, confronted, warned her daughter. What of the child? She had yelled. She is a daughter of the oak; it will bring nothing but sorrow, suffering.

She listened not. She had no care from her caution, but glared with a stranger's face, smirked, growled, as she had torn her faith from her neck, throwing it to the floor.

The crone had said no more. Though both had watched, as the silver symbol of their faith had fallen, lost, between the floorboards. She sighed as her old eyes scanned the floor for the dozenth time this night.

Still, the moon was ageing now, its cycle almost at an end. What was awaiting them with the new moon, she could only dread. The crone lingered by the leaded pane, her eyes boring through into the growing dawn. Fear lodged itself deep inside her chest, burrowing to her heart. She knew, with all that be good and holy, that this was the night.

†

Waiting patiently, with no hurried purpose, they were lingering 'til she is ready. Now, as the earth lay solid below her body, she could feel them rousing, stirring, calling to her with voices beyond her ears; they seeped through her skin, screaming from within her veins.

Her breath caught in her lungs, fixing her to the spot as the earth rumbled. It trembled, rustling the oak's leaves. Her face to the skies, debris fell, scattering her hair with agitated contempt, as the great oak wept.

Vast knotted roots shook off the damp soil as they coiled, twisting, filling the night air with sharp snaps and crunches. It consumed her ears, a thunderous roar. She closed her eyes as its cacophony played its own unique chorus, at one with the disembodied screams. Red sparks darted behind her eyelids, lightening her vision. Gripping the tree roots with bleeding fingers, she witnessed a tremendous rousing fog, soaring, reaching, rising from fierce orange flames. Dark shadows, swirling, with sharp talons of malevolent intent, began to reach up, gripping, taking her whole.

Her heart shattering into tiny fragments of splintered sorrow. The lightness she once knew, spent. Snuffed out, like an old candle, its wisped vapour, the last of her old self. Only darkness. For now, she was stronger. Her eyes soot-black, her skin shimmered. She lifted her palms to her face, turning them over; she wore a new skin.

She gazed up at the moon, broken by the mottled shade of the great oak, and smiled. She had watched the Goddess, each night for many, her full cycle, reflecting on her phases. She watched 'til; nothing remained of her heart.

She now knew its name. It was revenge.

Chapter Nine

'Something is coming, dear Mother…'

Manningtree - February 1ˢᵗ 1646

Wickedly cold. The afternoon was bitter. Its cloying chill sticking to all, dampness lingered in the beams. This winter had been harsh, never warming, the fire barely heating the chimney, the cottage held on to its kin with a clammy embrace.

As her old hands bolted the lock, the crone paused a moment, her forehead resting on the door.

'Mother, what is it? Who was that?'

'Another.' She heaved her head from the wood, standing straight, rubbing her lower back. She ached this day, maybe more than yesterday, maybe not, she could not tell. This winter's cold had seeped into her bones, slowly at first, almost without note, until she could barely remember a day she did not creak and squeak.

'Another? That be three in as many days. I will go.'

'No, daughter. I shall go this day. Thou must stay here, watch over your child. Besides, I need to rid my joints of this stiffness; walking will aid them.'

Gathering necessities, she left, the door slamming in her wake.

✝

Opening the coffer, she gathered another blanket. Carefully laying it, neatening the ends around the bed, she sat beside her daughter. Set her palm on the girl child's forehead. The fever gripped; it still held tight. She had done all that she knew, yet still, the fever had not waned.

Her heart ached at the sight. Her child, she could not lose her. She had watched as many had perished. Child after child. The village a veritable haven for the undertaker and stonemason. Small coffins laid in small graves. Children, infant and youth, cold and alone in the dark, no mother to hold their hands or smooth their brows. No comfort but the frozen earth.

She gripped her heart; it ached this day. Some days, she wondered if it even beat. However, this morn, as the sun in its bleak winter guise, had glared with its white shrill, piercing her chest. Casting a new sensation of fear into her, marking its ground, that maybe even she could not defeat what was coming.

'Mother?'

'Be still, my child.'

She teased the hair from the girl child's face, slick with sweat, the fever, ever close to the surface.

'I am here, my love. I shall always be by thy side.'

'I am afraid, Mother. I can feel it.'

'Hush. Sleep now, thou need rest.'

Fumbling for her mother, the child gripped her hand. 'Please do not leave me. Please stay.' Her grip was fierce. The mother gazed down as her hand whitened betwixt the child's grasp, her tiny fingertips drained of blood.

'Hush now, worry not, I shall stay right here, beside thee. Now, thou must sleep; thou will feel better for sleep.'

Carefully, she slackened the child's grip, settling her hands under the blanket for warmth. That thumping beat, deafening betwixt her ears. What to do? She knew the only course, the only remedy left to her. No matter what the consequence, did she have any other choice?

'Mother?'

'Rest now, I am but a stone's throw, by the hearth. Rest, and I shall make thee better.'

The girl child shook, her frail body quivered.

'Be at peace, my child, rest still.'

'Help me?'

Slowly at first, then, as it gained, the child's bed began to judder. Floorboards creaked, and the windowpanes shook.

She watched as her child rose, her body, her legs, raising the blankets from the bed. Her head slack, her long hair a tangled mass trailing on the pillow.

She placed her hands on the girl's shoulders, pushing her down, panic coursing through her veins.

Not her child, no, not her child. She would not lose her now. A great panic bellowed in the pit of her belly, she knew, but she denied. She would not allow it.

'NO', she yelled, the beams swallowing her voice. Again, she roared. Her words lost, snatched from the air as soon as they left her lips. She stood her ground, her eyes black, swirling tendrils of darkness dripping from her fingertips.

She growled.

The child's body dropped to the bed, still, motionless, her breathing faint, her heartbeat, the merest rhythm. The room calmed.

Her eyes, glazed, stared up at her mother's, reaching for her face. She gripped her daughter's hand, tightly holding onto life itself.

'My child?'

'They are coming for me, Mother.'

Chapter Ten

'Come, child, the darkness awaits.'

Manningtree - Samhain 1646

Darkness craved her. It desired nothing more than to drag her into the lingering wretchedness, to be swallowed by all that was sinful. She could feel it pulling, gradually ripping, shredding the fabric of her existence.

Though the room was small and humble, she felt their numbers, scores of them. Lurking. The girl child shuddered. Fear tiptoed down her arms as she clutched the blanket, tugging it up to her mouth. Wide-eyed, she searched the darkness as the shadows whispered those night chants.

They were here again this night, as they had been each night before. Had they always been there, waiting, observing 'til they deemed her ready? She could not recollect a night when they hadn't loitered in the dusty corners of her room. They beckoned to her, whispering her name as it travelled the wisps of night chill.

She considered the carved oak coffer at the foot of her bed, if it may perchance be the threshold through where they came, for they disappeared with sunrise.

'Grandmother, why is it so?'

'Child of mine own child,' the soft voice began as her grandmother placed a hand upon the child's forehead. 'The candle will keep light within thy heart. I light it this night as each before, to protect thy soul as thy mother's before,' she sighed heavily with the weight of deep sorrow. Gently, she placed the nightlight on the small bedside table with a clean handkerchief and a small cup of water.

The pewter stick held its white candle fast. The tall flame cast its glowing halo over the child's bed. Her tiny fingers released her covers, and they hovered to the light. She wondered if she could touch the flame. Would it burn? What of the pain; she often considered that. It flickered with the swishing of her small digits until quickly hiding them under the blanket once again.

†

Weariness had long since stolen all strength from the crone's legs. She heavily trod the wooden floorboards. These late vigils had taken their toll. Fatigued, she took rest upon the stool beside the window. Her old eyes traced the leaded glass; she checked the iron window latch, cold within her grasp. She had ensured its security at least a dozen times this night. For a moment, she contemplated her actions. It would not keep them out.

Beyond the cottage, beyond the garden, the lane, the trees, all that she knew existed by day had dissolved, devoured by the jowls of nightfall. Hadn't she known as dusk stroked the earth with its slithering fingers that this may be the night they came? Evil silently waiting in the beyond, the darkness. It pricked her thumbs with dread, the remembrance of those who had been taken before on a night such as this.

Her eyes sharpened on the landscape. She could sense it, feel it muse at her pain, hear it mutter her fears. It fed on her fear.

'Grandmother, please tell,' the girl swallowed the bitter lump that choked her still. 'Please tell of my mother.'

Her tiny fingers gripped the blanket in fists pressed to her cheeks, her knees tucked under her chin. Her grandmother closed her eyes, sighed heavily, her own hand going to where her amulet hung at her throat. Her twisted knuckles ached as she continually traced her thumb over its silver form.

'They came at night,' she began. 'They came swiftly on the night chill. Darkness carried them silently into our midst. Though she knew, your mother, she knew all too well that they hovered at our threshold. They waited. They watched 'til dawn rose above the chimney.'

Her trembling voice paused; she sniffed back the weight that had lain heavy within her soul. She stood, one hand resting firmly on the window ledge, the other intently about her pendant. The night was waning. She knew if she could just hold fast 'til dawn, sunrise would see the light steadfast in the child's soul. This night was to be the last; if she could believe and hold resolute 'til the break of morning, the child would be saved. Anxious how long she could hold this ritual, she glanced at the girl child huddled to the edge of the bed in the candlelight.

Her eyes: they were her mother's, that had always been the crone's fear. She had seen the glances, the expressions. The darkness that had consumed her mother would rise within them at nightfall. It hovered, just beneath the surface, bubbling, near to exploding in a deluge of merciless evil, taking the child with it.

The old woman pained at her memories; they had now taken both her children. She could hold fast; she was adamant she must. To lose this child would cast blackness in her own soul. To lose faith now would invite the devil.

'Grandmother?'

The old woman turned her back on the darkness and wandered toward the flickering candle. The girl shuffled across the bed; she sat, facing her as candlelight glowed betwixt them. She rubbed the girl's arm to pacify.

The child struggled to hold focus on her grandmother's face. The lurking shadows danced at the corner of her eye.

She could feel their fingers tug at her blanket; they were growing closer. Each night rising more powerful. This night, the child could sense her own soul slipping to darkness. They were coming for her.

Her fingers grappled to find her grandmother's. 'Do not let them come for me, Grandmother.' Her little body scrambled closer to her guardian, her thin back pressed hard against the carved headboard as her feet crawled beneath the woollen blanket. 'How am I to resist them?'

The crone steadily calmed the child's fingers. Tightly, she held her hands and her gaze.

'We shall hold fast and steady this night, for this be the final vigil. Goodness and light shall remain true and steadfast within thy young heart, child of mine own child. I shall not let any demon, living or other, from the shadows or the darkness, take thee this night or another.'

The girl child smiled, if only weary and tired. It touched the old woman's heart, making her resolve stronger for it.

'I wonder on the flame, Grandmother. Would it burn? Would it burn like fire?' her small voice quivered, as did the candle flame.

The old woman gasped at the girl's words. These many nights, weeks, and months, had she not protected her from the dark evilness that lurked in every corner of this damned place? She had done all within her power, such as it was, to keep the knowledge from the girl. To keep the light of protection glowing, as truth would bring darkness of the vilest kind.

She had promised to never speak of it, to keep the truth from her ears, for the truth would bring far more than knowledge. The truth would only entice evil from the shadows. No, she had promised. Always be sure to leave a candle burning.

Chapter Eleven

'A beauty, bound... but who will suffer?'

Manningtree - February 12th 1646

She tapped the glass.

'They hover in the field yonder. I sense them. Their presence strokes my aura with blood sodden hands. They think they hide; they cannot. My ears hear their heartbeats and smell their fear. They think I fear them. I do not, nor the evil that they do. Though, they fear me. I can taste it on their cold, dank breath. They come in numbers, at least a dozen men when I am but one woman. Oh, the folly of man and all that he believes to be so.

'May the tree roots arise from the earth this night, sharp and strong, creep amongst the tangled undergrowth. May they snatch them one by one into the earth, yanking their feet from beneath them. They shall be plucked, one each at a time, 'til none be standing. They shall lay, chin-deep within the frozen ground. Maybe they would welcome my presence to pull them free. But I will stand, raise my skirts in glee, and piss on their wretched faces. Oh, the folly of man, the evil that man does deserve no more,' she hissed with anger, shaking her head, running her fingers through her hair as if to rid them from her thoughts. 'No... I shall wait within this cottage, warm, whilst they linger in the freezing darkness, surrounded by their angst and piss rather than confront me this night.'

The woman flourished her hand over the window. The night's chill lined the cold panes with trailing fingers of frost. Her hand lingered on the latch, hesitating.

'Maybe, I should request their company, convey an invitation, let it carry across the frozen landscape in the form of...' she tapped her long finger on her cheek, then her hand glided down her neck to her breast, she sighed deeply as she let her head fall back. She stroked her throat and grinned. 'Oh, let me ponder. Ah... Ravens, with beaks as deadly as blades, let them peck eyes from skulls and tear flesh from bones. They shall do my bidding. We shall listen and dance to their cries. I would spare them the cold this bleak night, their bodies warmer for the blanket of blood.' A sly smirk found her full lips as she sniggered.

She glanced behind, a wry smile cutting her beautiful face. Her dark eyes sought out those of her mother. She found them in the threshold; her mother's face worn and tired.

'Hold fast thy foul tongue, girl. My ears ache at the din of thy shameful verse. Leave the window, and let the night be,' the crone scorned.

The woman's smile lingered on the countenance of her mother. The old crone slowly paced to the bed, where she leant down. The woman's eyes followed her into the room; her smile diminished with the sight of her child.

The small girl child lay sleeping in the vast bed. Her tiny frame curled, jumbled in the blanket of her mother's youth. The girl's pale face lay amidst the knotted strands of dark hair, a muss upon her pillow. She looked smaller than usual. The fever had waned, but she was far from safe; death remained sentry by her bedside, awaiting its claim.

The woman gazed upon her child, contemplated the prospect of death, her own, and that of her daughter. Maybe the reaper coming now for her pure soul would be the blessing they wished for. Would it save her daughter from her own fate? The woman was fully aware of what awaited her by sunrise. Dawn would bring finality; of that, she had no doubt. She had done what she needed to do; she was adamant of her choice.

The girl child, her child, was a stark reminder of the woman she once was. Perhaps she existed still beneath the dark shroud that had befallen her soul, blackening her heart. Somewhere, lingering in the darkness that now swam in the depths of her being, she remembered that spark of love. She had fought with the might of her ancestors to resist the shadows. But fear took her in the end, fear that latched onto the tail of her grief. Her now cold and empty core could not, nor would not, recall that grief; she had buried it deep in the hollow heart that once overflowed with love.

Turning back to the window, her fingernail tapped the leaded glass. It was *them* that had dug out her heart, as if with a pewter spoon, finally serving it to the shadows in corners. Those shadows she had strived with all her potency and integrity to resist. It was *them* she blamed. *Them* that had taken her sister, little more than a year ago, to have her life halted and cut short of womanhood.

Though it was no matter to them, with their evil deeds, that they would undertake in *his* name and the name of God. Nothing of his actions spoke of God, only of the devil himself. He roved these towns, these villages, reaping havoc on innocent folk. Purging the district of evil with acts of evil; what a mockery. With his boots, he trampled lives and fed on the fear of the weak and those willing to subscribe to his war. The General, he may call himself, a self-proposed title of cleansing. She laughed aloud at its irony. He gave the devil a bad name. His name carried only death in his wake.

She spat at the glass and those that waited beyond. The trail of saliva dribbled down the pane, halting on the leaded diamond in front of her eyes. She watched and laughed.

†

'They come, with cold bones in heavy boots. See how they tremble. The folly of man,' she mocked.

The old woman stood by the bed. 'I cannot save thee now, daughter,' she sorrowed as her bony fingers clutched her silver necklace. 'But by all that is good, we must hide the child!' She placed her old hand on the girl's forehead. 'The fever has broken, but she is weak still. Quickly. They come; we must hide her now, for I fear they will take her too.'

The woman looked from the window, her face still mocking and her eyes still dark. Once again, she cast them from her mother to her sleeping child.

A small beam of dawning light, pink with the blush of morning, cut through the window, bleeding brightness over the woman's dark hair. It touched her cheek. Holding fast on her eyes, they altered from darkest black to a golden brown. Her shoulders calmed. Her clenched fists eased. Her sharp features softened as pain shot an arrow of light dead between her ribs.

'Oh, mine own child!' she cried.

'Hasten thy step, daughter, time is waning, and we must act quickly.' The old woman pulled back the blankets, and tucking her arm gently beneath her granddaughter, heaved her up into her embrace. The fragile child lay small, weak and deathly still. 'Beneath, we shall have to hide her down there,' she urged.

Crouching and with a strong will of power, the woman pushed aside the carved bed and hurled back the woollen rug beneath. The trapdoor was small. She clasped the iron ring, and with true determination, pulled the handle. With a loud creak, the hinges gave way as the door opened.

'I shall take her down. Stay away from the window and be silent, I urge thee, keep thy tongue firm and good.'

The woman looked deeply into her mother's old eyes,

'They come to take me this day, of that there is no doubt. I shall not fear them now. I made a choice and did what was needed,' she smiled with sadness. She laid her palm over her child's face, 'May all that be good and pure keep thou safe, my child.' She kissed her pale cheek, 'for I love thee.'

Her thumping heart burned beneath her corset. She watched her mother descend the steep staircase, taking with her the only child she would bear, the part of her that had been her undoing. She could only wait. Time had run its course.

Her hand went to her throat. It was no longer there; at this moment, she wished for some faith. She had cast it off, ripping it from around her neck, as the darkness had shadowed her soul, smothering the light. She had watched the silver symbol tumble to the floor; had seen it and left it to fall and be lost between the floorboards.

The old woman heaved her aching bones from the opening, carefully letting the trapdoor shut, hiding away her grandchild.

'She sleeps, still with the effects of the fever; it may be hours 'til she awakes. A consolation, small but needed in the light of what awaits.'

'Keep my daughter safe.'

'Always,' the crone replied as they replaced the rug and hauled the bed back to the wall.

A thud.

A dull bang to the door, not of hands or fists, but something else—wood, clubs, sticks? The old woman breathed deeply and headed towards the threshold. Her daughter stepped in front, holding her shoulders, intent in her eyes as she motioned her to remain.

'I shall be the one to bring forward my end. Thou must stay safe within the walls of this cottage. Do not leave, for the safety of my child rests in thy hands from this moment forth.'

A silent tear struck her cheek, the first in a long time. She brushed it to her fingers and gazed upon it as if a strange unknown curiosity. Then, she smiled. 'The child is what good remains of my soul. Thou must save her, as thou could not save me.' Her beautiful smile shone, 'do not blame thyself for my wrongdoings. Thou tried with the power of light to save me. I love thee for it.'

Resolutely, she paced to the front door. Her fingers sprang the wrought iron latches. Again, a dull thump befell the sturdy wood.

'Open this door. Open it in the name of God,' a single voice yelled, and another thump to the wood.

She released the iron bar, the door swung open on its creaking hinges.

'Please, sir, cease hammering upon my door, for it is fit to splinter if thou persist. And with what would thou be pounding?' She paused at the sight of the tall, wiry man with a large leather bible in his grip.

'Ah… thou see fit to breach a gentlewoman's door with the word of the Lord. A mere knock would serve well at this early hour, sir. Look, the dawn has scarcely arisen above the rafters. It is certainly not the hour to be of bellowing voice or a thumping bible, does thou not agree?' The woman could not help but revel in derision and irony.

The clergyman stood alone. The local do-gooders hovered in the lane beyond; fierce façades worn upon the band of fearful men.

'Be of silent tongue, woman.' The reedy man stepped forward; his foot heavy upon the stone threshold.

She glanced down at his leather boot caked in sodden mud. She turned her head to the side, sniffed deeply, as she cast her eyes from his feet, up his legs, to the white-collar of his faith, and finally to his face. It was thin, gaunt, and bleak around his eyes. His hair lay tangled and damp beneath his hat, drips of the dawn moisture dewy upon his withered cheeks. Her nose wrinkled at the smell of damp earth and piss.

'I contemplate from the sight and smell of thy attire that thou must have spent the night with the owls and slept sound and homely beside the vermin. What be the foulness that reeks from thy clothes? A gentleman of God and goodness should surely keep better of thyself. Cleanliness being of Godliness, sir.' Her lips smiled lightly, full and plump, the colour of sweet plums. She licked them gently as her eyes softened on his. 'Please, gentle sir, would thou remedy thy boots of the damp earth before thou consider placing a foot upon my step.'

The man looked down at his boot resting on the worn stone, slowly retracting his foot. His cold eyes carried up the woman before him, her brown woollen skirts, her tight corset the shade of burnished autumn, the dark hair that lay tousled about her shoulders, and her skin. His eyes lingered on her milky skin. He stood static, mesmerised by the gentle rise and fall of her bosom, the blush, the plumpness of her breasts as they swelled, overflowing the confines of her corset. He licked his chapped lips in reflection of hers as his eyes carried to her full mouth.

For a moment, he could think of nothing but the sudden want and desire that boiled within him. To take his hand and plunder beneath her petticoats, to find what warmth lay within, to taste the sweetness of her flesh, to rip the corset from her breasts and run his tongue over those milky mounds. To ravage her mouth with his. A hand left his bible, tugged eagerly at the aching that swelled in his breeches. Within seconds, his eyes widened with sheer horror, almost dropping the good book as his mind crashed with the weight of solemnity.

She smiled.

'Bitch!' he cried. 'With what evil do thou curse a man of the cloth?'

'Sir, it is nothing but the true desire that dwells within all men. Do not cast accusations upon my womanhood if it offends or coaxes a man's eyes. Are thou not a man? I am but a woman. Do not all men desire a woman? Am I not a woman to be desired, sir?' she taunted.

'Enough!' he shrieked. 'Seize the Witch!'

✝

Bright winter rays formed shards of light over the rooftops, thatch and tile. Great splinters of midday sun needled her cheeks. She cursed them. She cursed the warmth. She cursed the hope the midday sun once granted. She cursed its relentlessness.

Coarse chafing rope scuffed and grazed her ankles; blood, both fresh and congealed upon its weave. They had bound her tight. Her hands clenched together hopelessly behind her. The rope, thick with great knots, gouged her skin. The rope about her throat made movement slight; she could barely turn. The back of her head pushed hard against a great lumber of wood. A tree from the yonder coppice.

The town square was filling with jeering local folk. She recognised faces; some she knew well, women she had aided in childbirth. More faces appeared. They were strange to her eyes. She knew that folk would trek from other villages and hamlets. She had known it far too often. They had come to watch, travelled to witness his success. He relished their presence, making a spectacle of his findings, proof of his ability to punish the vileness that loitered. This would ensure his further employment. They bestowed him great faith to rid their towns of evil.

He stood before her now. His tall boots polished and buckled, his black cloak long about his shoulders, somehow represented his self-appointed title. His doublet and breeches pristine, and his hat resting upon his righteous head. He was a young man of no more age than her. She had seen his posters, the pamphlets with his likeness, she mocked at the thought, almost a parody of himself. A far cry from the boy she had once known. He would never have lain in wait all night to come by dawn. He had sent his sycophants, eager to do his bidding, to gain favour and to bask in the shine of his glory. She scorned at the sight of him. She scorned her own heart.

'So, thou are here within the confines of my rope, at last, Witch.' With steepled fingers set to his lips, he patted his mouth in rhythmic time, humming as he went. 'Had thee thought I had forgotten?' She did not move nor gesture to his question. He had not expected an answer. He was toying with her; she being the entertainment this day. 'Are thou wondering why thou are here, Witch?' he shuffled on the spot, hands now behind his back as he rocked back and forth on his heels. Oh, he was of true arrogance.

She stared down into his eyes. She could see it as clear as the white sun that hung in the bitter winter sky. Terror oozed from his pores. This grand façade of righteous dignity, of good-doing, was just that, a façade. This was a man, an average man, a God-fearing man, with no significant ability or right to accuse or question than the lowly farmer in the following field. His reputation lay before him, devastation in his wake. Roaming, touting the countryside for employment, claiming to own a gift of insight, inquest to pursue innocent womenfolk, those that served only to aid the ill and infirm, to take said women and claim them to be Witch. Some maiden, some crone, age was of no consequence. And he was revered. He conveyed an air of solemnity and honour about his person.

She gazed intently into his face as the darkness swelled in her belly. The evil that she was eager to suppress by day rose into an immense swirling mist of malevolent intent. She was to die this day, by the hand of her enemy, and the townsfolk were to watch and cheer at his triumph, the great Witchfinder General.

She spat at his face, a great glob of frothing spittle falling short, landing clear of his boots. He advanced with precise footsteps until his feet met the kindling and firewood that formed the great pyre. She stood above him amid the pile, lashed to the immense wooden stake. She glared down at him, her eyes darkened, her skin of pale luminescence, almost the white of her linen shift, her dark hair loose about her shoulders and breast.

'Thou see, I prepared something special for thee?'

'A spectacle?'

'No less than thou deserve.'

'Should I be flattered?'

'Hanging is too good, too easy. Too quick'

'Oh, Matthew.'

'How dare thee speak with such familiarity.'

'Has thou forgotten the intimacy we once shared?'

'Enough!' he barked, waving his arm fiercely towards a man behind him.

'Matthew, this will be thy undoing. I promise thee.'

'Thou shall be dead before sun fall.'

'I shall remain inside thy head. Thou shall see my face in thy sleep. Thou shall feel my hands on thy body and awake to wish it so.'

'Devil's Whore.'

'That is not the name thou once called me.'

'Witch!' he yelled. 'Now, man, I will wait no longer. Light it. Light it now. I shall watch this witch burn this day!'

Chapter Twelve

Is it possible for the night to be so dark?

So overwhelming you can feel your soul being plucked from your body and every ounce of happiness sucked through your pores?

I shudder.

It is beyond dark. A dense blanket, a thickness hangs in the air—almost suffocating. I've never known blackness like it. My eyes follow the windscreen up beyond the steering wheel. I lean forward, pressing my boobs against it, peering under the visor into the night sky. The word *night* feels wrong somehow; it's as if the world has just ceased to exist. Unsettlingly heavy, I can feel it; evil is still here, evil followed me home tonight.

But here we are, driving back.

There are no streetlights on this stretch of road, the long winding route through the Suffolk and Essex countryside. The road gently undulates through the trees from village to village. I muse over the lack of stars. Where is the moon? Where is life? I've watched the Twilight Zone; we've driven into a parallel world dominated by the supernatural. I laugh at the irony.

The glow of the orange digits on the dashboard annoys my peripheral vision—3.00 am. I'm a marionette to my nerves; they have me dangling. I can feel my blood sting under my skin. It's the strangest sensation, as if my anxiety is poisoning me from within.

We drive in silence, as silent as my car allows; the clunking and grinding from the back is utterly annoying at best. But tonight, my possessed car has switched up the volume control. How inconsiderate. I must get that brake disk replaced.

'Heather, I can't believe you are driving this damn effing car like this!' Alex scorns my arse. 'It'll be the death of you or me tonight. So irresponsible.'

'Don't moan. I'll get it done this week; it's been parked up for the past month. Not my fault you were low on petrol.' I glance across. He's cracking his knuckles again.

'I didn't have time on my way to pick you up, not my fault your petrol station closes at midnight!' He sighs, a loud crackling moan.

He's nervous; I can hear it, not in his voice but in the vibrations his body is sending my way. Shock waves are bombarding me. I bloody hate it when that happens. As if I'm not stressed enough without Alex's tension to boot. He's usually so calculated, systematic, professional. And he never swears; effing's about as close as we ever get to it. Unlike me, I 'swear like a trooper,' my dad used to say. It's understandable, though, after tonight. My heart sends a sloppy, sympathetic kiss to his.

We have been in this situation before; it would be a blatant lie to say we haven't. Although, I'm thankful that we've never been called back in the middle of the night until now. Yup, I sigh; this is the first cause of my agitation. Not the late hour so much as the call itself. There was something wrong in her voice, not just shaken or afraid, but something else I can't put my finger on. But no point worrying about it now. We just need to get there in one piece in this bloody car.

I look over to Alex as if he's about to open his mouth. His Samsung illuminates his lap; he has the case file open across his jeans; typical Alex, always on it. Just a mass of shorthand scribbles; it's yet to be typed up. I never did learn how to scribble; my regular handwriting is sufficiently illegible.

'Heather.'

I'm looking straight at him, but still, I jump out of my skin as my name breaks the silence and seems to almost break the darkness too. Then I realise it's not Alex. He is still riffling through his biro scrawlings.

'Heather.'

Then the big clunking penny drops. The witching hour always plays havoc with my nerves. I full-on cackle to myself as I gaze back at the clock. Alex laughs automatically despite himself, a knee jerk reaction.

'Heather, what is it? Something's up.'

'Understatement of the millennia, I'd say. But yes. Angelina,' I laugh again, this time more of a stressed squeak. 'I thought it was you; she made me jump.'

'Heather, everything is wrong. Tread carefully; it's not as it should be… I thought it was over,' I recite her words to Alex, he shrugs.

'Honestly, after what we saw this evening, I'm not sure that's really enlightening or rather stating the obvious,' he grumbles and goes back to his notes.

'I'm only repeating the message.'

I fidget in my seat, the darkness, or rather the lack of light is beginning to get under my skin, making me itch. I take a huge breath, shaking my shoulders as I exhale. Okay, we can do this. Maybe there is something I've missed. I don't do defeat, I don't do 'oh well, better luck next time.' This isn't a game; this is people's lives. I'm a professional.

It almost feels like I'm driving blind. I know the headlights are on and working fine; it's the brakes that are dodgy. But no matter how I concentrate, it's as if the darkness is sucking all the light out of my bulbs. The road in front is almost black. I pull over. I know what's coming from Alex now. We should have driven to get petrol and gone in his car. There was no time. The call was so… well, not just urgent but panic-stricken. I shudder again, remembering the sound of her voice. I pull on the handbrake.

I hold my shaking finger on the button. As the window slides down, a sudden rush of cold air hits my face. I close my eyes, leaning my head out as far as my seatbelt will allow. Opening my eyes, it's so dark they could still be shut; I blink to check. No, they are open. It's just ridiculously dense like a blanket of fog. I reach out, my arm straight as I flex my fingers. No fog.

'Why have we stopped? You, ok? What's the matter with the car?' Alex looks up bleary-eyed, so absorbed by his notes.

'Can you feel it?'

'What? What's the matter?'

'Just put the papers down a min and look. Look outside.'

Alex opens his window and leans out into the night. A through breeze rushes into the car between us, from one window to the other.

I'm not easily frightened, wouldn't be good in my line of work, but I swear, it's like fingers tickling then grabbing at my face and arms—clawing me.

'Shut it! Shut the bloody windows now!' I cry.

I'm shaking all over. Even my toes in my trainers are shivering.

'Hey, calm down. It's fine.' His finger is closing window as he speaks. I can't close mine quickly enough, and I fumble. Why is everything on go-slow when you're in a hurry? I watch as my window reaches the top rubber seal. I hear myself sigh.

'Ok…' Alex softens, 'now, slowly, tell me what's got you all bothered? This isn't really your thing. I don't understand why you're so spooked, Heth.'

'The darkness, Alex, just look at it. Can't you see it, don't you feel it?'

'Heather, it's dark outside, of course, it's effing dark outside, it's the middle of the night. But calm down, it's normal…' he glances out the window, leaning forward, looks up under his visor into the sky above. 'Okay, so there's no moon that I can see, odd I admit, but it's the countryside, and there aren't any effing streetlights in the middle of the bloody countryside.' He pauses, watching my face. He's frowning. 'Heather, you're as white as a bloody sheet.' He presses his palm to my forehead. 'Eh… you're all clammy too.' I can see his face, shadowed in the light from his lap. His phone is pointing directly up under his chin. He looks slightly worried now. 'Okay, get out the bloody car; I'm driving now. You're in no fit state, probably no fitter than this effing car of yours,' he demands and undoes his belt. I can hear him swearing under his breath.

I dash around the car. Honestly, it's no word of a lie; if this were a movie, there'd be some awful prowling demon or monster lurking behind these trees. I scrambled to get back in the car, hitting my hip on the boot in my rush—*shit!* I'm in. I manage to gather his notes together from under my butt and the ones I've scattered in the footwell. I rest my head back, my eyes close, my pounding heart sending its beating rhythm through my whole body like a drum. Alex starts the car and pulls away.

Okay, I'm a big girl, I know how fear can take hold, and I've seen it happen so often. I'm normally the calm one, reassuring the panicked others. I know this is more than just being afraid of the dark. I'm not even sure the dark has anything to do with it, no matter how odd it all feels out there. I'm taking huge breaths, deep, calming breaths; I've read a few books on meditation, took a class or two in my time, so that seems the obvious thing to do. I just need to gather my shit together. I have a job to do.

'How long before we arrive?' I ask in a husky voice that seems to belong to someone else. I cough to clear the choking lump.

'About twenty minutes or so. If we were in my car, I'd go a little fast as there's no traffic, but I just daren't risk it in this,' he smiles. 'I'm teasing, don't worry, I'll get us there in one piece; it'll be about 3.30 am.'

The best I can do is go over everything that happened this evening. Maybe there is something I missed; there must be. The call was wrong; it all feels so wrong. I had done what I'd set out to do. They were okay when we left—just about!

I close my eyes again. I need more information, help from Angelina. But she's quiet.

Chapter Thirteen

Manningtree - October 31st 2016

The journey to Manningtree was normal.

There was nothing odd or out of the ordinary except for a niggling feeling in the pit of my stomach. My brain went over each detail—my ritual. We'd remembered everything, our usual bag of tricks, as Alex called them. I'd even worn my lucky knickers. The weather had a chill, generally like any other autumn evening. Halloween, the date hadn't escaped me. Not a night I usually work, I must admit.

As we approached the town centre, I heard it. That was it, that niggle and the one thing that I dreaded, the words that always manage to put me on edge, even after all this time. Alex looked at me with his predictable please-don't-say-it expression.

'I know you don't want to hear this, but…' I hesitated for a second, just to make sure I'd heard it right.

'Oh no, Heather! Just for once, it'd be nice to have a straightforward one. You're exhausted. It's been one of those weeks,' he sighed as we stopped at some traffic lights.

I knew Alex was only thinking of me, but after all these years we've worked together, he knew there was nothing I could do about it. After all, I'm just the messenger, the interpreter if you like; my job is only to pass it on.

'Hey, I know you never signed up for an easy ride.' I smiled at him.

'Hey, when I signed up, I'm not sure I had any real idea of

what sort of a ride it was going to be—easy or not,' Alex replied with a smile to mine.

Within a few minutes, we'd arrived. It was 6.15 pm. It was dark. The house sat in a conventional Victorian terrace, much like the others in the street, house after house with bay windows and glossy painted doors.

As we got out of the car, I grabbed my bag, and my feet found the solid pavement beneath them. My heart was pounding. Uneasy anxiety spread through my body—pull yourself together. Alex locked the car; the mechanical click made my teeth grate. With a low voice, tugging my sleeve slightly, I turned to Alex as he asked me exactly what I had expected.

'Heth, just before we go in, what did you hear?'

'Only, we have to be on our guard. It's not all as it seems. Nothing more than that, but it was very adamant.' I smiled at Alex. However, he could see it in my face. 'She's never let me down, Alex; I trust her emphatically.'

'I know you do… and I trust you!'

I grasped the door knocker as I took a deep breath and a private prayer for a peaceful one—unlikely.

'Hello, you must be Heather and Alex. I'm Dawn.'

Dawn was young and pretty, though she appeared old beyond her years. I knew she was only in her twenties, but she looked so harassed.

'This is the lounge, obviously… as you can see, sorry,' she announced. Her unease apparent on her face, nerves made her shudder as she continually scratched the skin around her fingers. 'Sorry, I know that was a silly thing to say, I'm… I'm just a bit nervous, that's all,' she whispered, leaning into me so close her hair tickled my cheek.

'It's fine, don't worry,' I replied, trying to put her at ease.

My nose was bombarded by an overpowering smell of perfume, cheap and sweet, but not totally unpleasant.

Probably an overindulgent dose to compensate for the lack of bathing, as her hair lay a lank, greasy mass down her back. That bad, eh?

She twitched as she gripped my arm, almost unwilling to let go. I pulled away slowly so as not to alarm her; she smiled, then her eyes stared past me up the hallway. Her face sank into a state of panic. I could hear her gulp; her eyes quickly darted back to me; her stare intense. I took her hands and held them in mine. Her apprehension smothered her, and I could feel her shake under my touch. I turned her hands over. She had red raw patches around her long nails from her continued scraping; they were still bleeding. Her sweater sleeves were pushed up to the elbow, exposing swollen patches, almost like grip marks or maybe blisters.

I looked into her pale face, clearly starved of rest. Dark shadows under her eyes made them deep-set and sad.

'Let's get to it Dawn, the sooner we get started, the sooner you can sleep. Who else is coming?'

'My sister's here; she's in the kitchen making some tea and coffee. That's okay, isn't it?' her face looked stricken, '…and my mother.'

I turned over my shoulder to see Alex, bag in hand with his back to the front door; he nodded.

'Sounds fantastic, that's great, two coffees both white no sugar. And Dawn, don't worry. We shall do our best to put this house at peace. Trust me.'

'I hope so,' she leant in to whisper in my ear; I shuddered again. 'I hope so, Heather, I really do. I hope I can trust you.'

There was a dark essence in that sentence that made my teeth clench. I put it down to her nerves. Although, I couldn't help but feel there was something she wanted to say or ask. I didn't reply; I simply nodded and smiled. I wasn't exactly sure what I could say. So Alex and I followed Dawn down the hall into the kitchen.

The room was bright and airy thanks to an extension that swept the house back, at least the same depth again of the original building, resulting in a great, open-plan space. I must admit, I had slight pangs of the green-eyed monster, as I could almost fit my whole tiny cottage into this room.

'Hi, Heather? I'm Denise, but please call me Deni. It's great to finally meet you and put a face to a voice, so to speak. Coffee?'

Deni was undeniably Dawn's sister, pretty and smelling of fading Channel No.5. It had been her that made the first contact. She'd found us via a friend of a friend, apparently, although the names never rang a bell. Some people don't like to admit they had to actually search for paranormal investigators in Google.

She gripped my hand in an over-excited shake. 'We're eager to get this all over with, you know, it's been such a long time. To finally end it... so my poor sister can get life back to normal.' She smiled again; this time, there was an underlying pain there. 'It's been months now. As you can see,' she lowered her voice and gestured towards her sister, now sitting at the central island. 'She's just about had as much as she can take. She came to stay with me for a few days, but it made no difference. She never slept, couldn't sleep and was so eager to get back here,' she shrugged.

'We shall do our best,' I answered with a nod as I took in the sight of Dawn, head in her hands, almost as if covering her ears. She was rocking gently, mumbling to herself.

I stood taking in the whole room, my eyes quickly darting around to see a woman standing with her back to a door, a cupboard, maybe the original pantry. The mother, I presumed. She was watching me. I'm not sure how long she'd been there; I hadn't noticed her but certainly hadn't seen her arrive either. Her dark hair hung quite long over her shoulders, and although obviously the girls' mother, she wasn't very old or certainly had aged quite well. I glanced over to the sisters and then back again; she must be in her fifties. I hoped I could look that good at fifty.

'Coffee, Heth.' Alex nudged my arm as I saw Deni holding two mugs. I took my proffered coffee and headed to the central island. Alex sat beside me, the sisters opposite. I couldn't take my eyes from the mother as she very slowly came to sit down next to Dawn.

'Oh, this is our mother, Margaret… Maggie,' Deni smiled and handed her mother a cup of tea.

'Hello Maggie, I'm Heather, and this is my colleague, Alex.' I offered my hand, but she wasn't having any of it.

She looked at my hand and up at my face as if I was an alien. Talk about cold. I was clearly unwelcomed in her eyes. Some people are just sceptical. That's fine with me; I can't expect everyone to believe or understand.

That was basically the crux of it. I come across so many people who, because they can't, or don't want to understand, then it can't really be happening, therefore I'm a fraud, and this is all fake. Those people just need to find a rational explanation for these things. It's all fine with me. I don't judge anyone's opinions. After all, and it's still laughed about, when Alex came to work with me, he was very much the scientific bod with a rational viewpoint. That may have changed somewhat over the years, he's now more 'open-minded' as he says, but he won't admit he's a full believer. He needs to keep one foot in the sceptic field rather than jumping straight over the fence.

We hugged our mugs. Maggie sipped her tea from her china teacup. She hadn't taken her eyes off me. It was quite unnerving. She'd not spoken a word, not to me, nor her daughters. I was beginning to question if it was more than nerves if she was afraid. Her expression was blank. It wasn't just cold; it was more than that. It was vacant.

My mind wandered to my childhood; I'd seen an expression like that before. Growing up, we'd lived next door to an elderly pair of spinster sisters. I always hated that word spinster—unmarried sisters. They were lovely, very chatty, and always baking. You could smell it all the way up the street in the summer. As they got older, one of them became frequently forgetful. We had the fire brigade out once for a kitchen fire, and I'd often find her roaming the park when she'd taken her long-since dead dog for a walk and forgotten the way home.

As I looked at Maggie now, that is what it reminded me of. Her expression was not so much cold as forgetful, dementia of some kind. I hate labels. But there was something about this woman. My heart instantly ached, awful. This woman was of no age to deteriorate.

Now, I didn't know; I was speculating. I was making assumptions, dangerous things. Deni hadn't said anything regarding their mother; she hadn't been mentioned at all. Maybe she wasn't expecting her to attend tonight. Either way, I wanted to reach out and touch her hand, reassure her somehow. But as I looked into her eyes, I thought better of it. I didn't want to highlight it as an issue. She made me shudder.

Alex took out his notepad and biro while I asked Dawn to recite the month's events. She did so with a little coaxing, poor girl, and with the aid of Deni with the odd 'oh don't forget' and 'oh remember when' as she idly rubbed Dawn's arm. It was evidently an affectionate sisterly gesture; she wasn't even aware of it. Dawn still had her head down, occasionally covering her ears. Alex took notes, and I listened, taking it all in, making my mental notes. I wasn't the only one listening.

Angelina was with me. She's always with me.

Chapter Fourteen

We were ready.

The dining room had been identified as the most affected, with all the major activities and disturbances. We headed back down the front hallway, the dining room being opposite the lounge, a bay window facing the front road.

Once Alex opened the door, we were confronted by a heavy feeling of pressure, almost dread. The room was colder than the rest of the house. The infrared thermometer displayed a variant of four to five degrees lower than the hallway. Nevertheless, with his standard scientific approach, Alex put it down to the curtains being closed and the afternoon light that had been flooding the hallway. I had to agree with him. He set up the night vision camera on its tripod, pointing to take in most of the room.

Bloody hell, it was cold in there.

As a dining room, it was much like any other. Built-in cupboards, display shelves on either side of a chimney breast housed china ornaments, books and general stuff. Now all covered in a thick layer of dust. There was a large mirror above the marble fireplace that faced the door and a round dining table and chairs in the centre of the room.

I placed my bag on the floor and pulled out a white cloth; it billowed and came to rest on the table. I went around the table, easing out the dining chairs, spacing them evenly. I planned to sit Dawn opposite the door on the other side, not that I expected her to make a dash for it, not that you can't be too careful, but because it was the perfect view for the night vision camera set up. I would sit opposite her, my back to the door, Deni and Maggie on either side. Back to my bag, I retrieved my candle and matches. Centrally on the table, I placed a thick white candle, securing it on its little silver plate.

The ladies hovered, watching intently from the doorway. Dawn gripped the doorframe, white-knuckled, her head leaning against it. She was clearly shaking. Deni had her arm tucked under hers, whispering gently in her ear to coax her in. Maggie, on the other hand, stood behind, closer to the lounge door, her arms folded, her shoulders square, and her face rather than being blank now had an air of defiance about it. I must admit she made me nervous. I almost wished I'd said something earlier. Maybe, she would have been better leaving.

'It's time, ladies if you please.' I gestured to the table. Dawn hesitantly approached, and I guided her to the seat. Deni to my left and Maggie to my right, furthest in the room. I smiled at each in turn. Dawn didn't really see me; she had her head down again, poor girl. Deni replied with an anxious smile and almost squealed, whilst Maggie quietly sat without so much as a murmur, silent as the grave, that one — excuse the pun.

Alex lit the candle. Time was getting on. He switched off the light, taking a position with the thermal imaging unit about two feet behind me; he uses this to pick up any cold or hot spots that may occur; he can record them for later reference.

Alex isn't my assistant; he's my partner, not only my chauffeur, my backup, but my rock and my bodyguard, well, so to speak, although it's not my body that's at risk. He has an academic ability that allows him to adopt a scientific view on the events with the meter reading from the EMF, and he takes notes of any information so that we can analyse it later.

I cleared my throat, glanced over at each of my companions and began. 'Now, ladies, we all need to place our hands flat on the table before us and link our little fingers; this creates a circle. We must not break the circle. Please, you cannot remove your hands or break the link between us no matter what may occur. Do you all understand?'

Again, I looked at each in turn to reiterate the importance. I hesitated a moment and then began.

'Are there any passed on souls who wish to make contact? If you can hear my voice and wish to speak to us, make yourself known.'

There was nothing. The room remained silent. I gazed over at Alex for some sort of acknowledgement. He simply shook his head—nothing.

'Are there any spirits here who would like to make themselves known to us? We are here to make contact.'

Now, I know it sounds clichéd, like something out of a cheap scary movie, so I wasn't the least surprised when Deni started to laugh. She looked mortified with herself; I just smiled, nodded, and continued.

A shudder travelled the length of my back. I knew someone had brushed past me. The temperature dipped as the flame flickered. I watched it for a moment as the flame danced. It elongated twice its length and swayed from side to side. The atmosphere altered. The darkness intensified, with all attention on the candle flame. The coldness attacked my face. At that moment, it was so intense I couldn't ever remember being so cold.

'Oh, what was that?' announced a somewhat nervous voice. Deni fidgeted in her seat, her hands shaking as she tried to keep them firm on the cloth. 'Someone just touched my shoulder!' she cried, 'I'm not sure I like this!'

'Don't be afraid. There is a woman here, a young woman. No, it's a girl,' I attempted to reassure her and took a deep breath. 'What is your name spirit, can you make the candle flicker again for us?'

The frosty chill that was stroking my face moved around the table, touched the other's cheeks in turn as an icy hand moved from face to face. Then, the inevitable, a chain reaction of terror, swept the table. First, Deni jumped in her seat, her hands falling away from the circle as she clutched her face to rid the ghostly hands. This made poor Dawn even more flustered, as she too screamed and burst into tears, although her hands remained glued to the cloth. She shook, and so did the table along with her.

Even I, after all these years, was seized by my fear. I was desperately trying to stay calm, deep breaths in and out to focus my energy. The last thing I wanted was to lose control of this room, the girls, or this spirit—whoever she was. She had caused enough trouble in this house, she had now come forward, and I had invited her to do so.

Inviting mayhem in is never a great situation to be in.

In my head, I was calling to Angelina. I was beginning to feel a little abandoned by her, to be honest. She was always by my side, on the other side, that is. She was, after all, my spirit guide. I was calling her. I had been calling her since we had entered the room.

'Angelina, please. I need some idea of what I'm dealing with.'

'Sorry, Heather, she is blocking me. She has been blocking me all evening. I can't see who she is; she is shrouded. But be warned, she is not all she seems.' Fab!

It took a few minutes to regain some peace and order around the table. The girls, although terrified out of their wits, had sat calmly again—sort of—and linked fingers to gather the circle together. I had been so flustered with the girl's commotions; I had only just looked at the mother.

Maggie hadn't moved. She sat perfectly calm, her hands restful and flat on the tablecloth. She didn't look at me, though. I noted that she had all her attention fixed on Dawn. I couldn't see in this light if she wore an expression of any kind; all I knew was that she hadn't been fazed by the ghostly chill or bout of hysterics. She appeared defiant.

'Come forward again, spirit. What is your name?' I gestured to Alex; as he wandered the table with the thermal imager, he shook his head. There was no fluctuation.

I carefully repeated my request twice more.

'My name be Sarah.'

I looked dead in front of me. The room was dark, all but the candle flame which cast strange shapes and shadows to our faces.

'My name be Sarah.' The words came again. They were coming from Dawn's mouth, her head up, her eyes intently open and fixed upon my face.

'Hello, Sarah,' I replied, with my gaze set on Dawn's face. 'We mean you no harm. We wish to help you.'

'Help me?' Dawn's lips were moving, but her face was static and steady like a ventriloquist's dummy as if only her chin could respond. Her eyes bore into mine, sharp and clear over the candle flame. I straightened my back on the chair, my fingers gripping those on either side of me. The candle flame blew back and forth between us as the white cloth rippled around the table in an undulating wave of movement over our thighs.

'We can help you cross over, Sarah, to go into the light.'

'Go into the light?'

'Yes, Sarah, you are not of this plane anymore. You belong in the light; we are here to guide you across.'

'The light?' the words were whispered across the table as Dawn gently leant forward towards me. Her eyes now had a look about them—intuitiveness. She leant forward a little.

'That's not her voice,' squeaked Deni through gritted teeth. 'That's not her voice! It sounds wrong. It sounds... like a child. I don't understand?' She began to weep. I squeezed her fingers to ease her.

'It's okay. The spirit is using her as a channel; she is using her energy to speak to us.'

I fixed my eyes on Dawn's face, examining her features, hunting for a hint of the spirit, for some idea of Sarah's identity—her intentions. I was still asking Angelina, but no help there. It felt as if Angelina was having her own problems with this one.

'Come, Sarah, come forward. How old are you? What year did you pass over?' My voice must have exhibited my uneasiness as I asked my routine questions, and I could feel it break.

'Pass over?'

'Sarah, what year is it?'

Dawn's expression was one of bewilderment. She sat back in her chair, her eyes still directed at me. Then she began to sway, body gently gliding from side to side, hands pressed to the table. She bowed her head over her chest, with her lank hair touching the cloth. We could hear muttering; Dawn was muttering something. I couldn't make out the words; it was as if she were whispering or chanting to herself. Either way, she was getting agitated. The swaying became greater, the muttering slightly louder. Her greasy hair was sweeping across the surface of the cloth.

'1646,' she mumbled under her breath, '1646.'

I took hold of the room, the table, and the job in hand.

'How old are you, Sarah? Did you die in 1646?' my voice almost boomed across the table. Deni was weeping quietly to herself, obviously trying to hold it together. Maggie, on the other hand—literally—was calm, with just her stare fixed on Dawn.

'The light is no longer. I cannot see the light… only dark,' Dawn whispered from beneath her hair, 'they came for me.'

'She is but a girl child.'

My body froze. Slowly, very slowly, I looked to my right as a great rush of goosebumps scuttled like ants down my back. Maggie was staring at me. Her eyes were wide and wild. Her body firm and steady. Oh, bloody hell!

'A child. She is but a girl,' Maggie's voice, despite the rigidity of her posture, was soft and beguiling, like a melody around the table. It swept in a gentle breeze to my ear as she kept repeating over and over. 'She is but a child. My child.'

These were the first words she'd spoken the whole evening. And to be honest, I wasn't sure if they were hers at all. There was a strange oldness about them, about her phrasing and repetition. And how the hell did she know that Sarah was a child? Or did she mean Dawn? Was it her motherly instinct, kicking in during a time of crisis? A sudden act of clarity? I had no idea.

I looked directly at Maggie. 'What is your name, spirit? Is Sarah your child?'

'They took me first.'

'Who took you?'

I glanced over at Dawn. She still swayed in her seat, her hair swishing the cloth, Muttering or weeping. I couldn't quite tell. It was high pitched. I turned quickly back to Maggie. Her face had a knowing now, her expression, lost.

'They took me. Then they came for my child.'

Her head fell forward. She sat perfectly still. Then turned and stared at Dawn.

Chapter Fifteen

The room was now bloody freezing. My hands were like ice. I wasn't sure I could move them if I tried; they felt numb, superglued to the cloth. I gathered my breathing, trying to calm myself. I exhaled, my breath a ghostly mist before my face.

'Sarah,' I began gently. 'How old are you, Sarah? How old are you? Please don't be afraid; we mean you no harm, only to help you.' Okay, I was doing quite well; my inner self, although quaking in my trainers, outwardly seems quite together. 'My name is Heather. Tell me yours.'

'Heather,' Dawn repeated lightly as if calling from a great distance.

'The light has gone, Heather.' With that, Dawn looked up, so quickly she took me completely by surprise, and I jumped back, jogging the table. The flame flickered as the candle wobbled. She was looking at the candle now. 'The light has gone.' She then smiled.

Oh, that was creepy as hell! Dawn hadn't smiled all evening. And this sure as hell wasn't a natural one either. Her teeth glowed in the candlelight; her eyes twinkled, not with delight but more disdain.

Eager to look away a moment, I looked at Alex. He was standing directly behind Deni, his thermal imager fixed on Dawn, then Maggie; I could see his hand guiding from one to the other. He looked at me. I was waiting for him to speak. He said nothing, just stood open-mouthed. He quickly headed to me, pushing the imager in front of my nose; I edged my head back to focus. It was still facing the women as he moved it gently from Maggie to Dawn, and I could see the cause of his gawping. The room was blue, bright blue to show its freezing temperature, just as I was expecting. The women, on the other hand, were vivid red shapes sat at the table. To give an idea, the candle's flame at its hottest point was yellow, barely orange. These women were burning hot. I gestured my head for him to point it at Deni; she was a shade of yellow with cold extremities, her hands blue, much the same as my own. Only Dawn and Maggie looked like they had central heating.

With a quick whip, Dawn removed her hands from the cloth, her fingers hovering over the candle. Slowly, again, her body gently swayed from side to side, her head lolling on her shoulders and her fingers playing with the flame. She leant closer. I could see the flame flickering in her eyes as they stayed intent on mine. Her fingers were literally playing with the flame; she'd have some sore burns tomorrow, I thought. Oh, bloody hell; we have to get through tonight first.

I must admit, I was glued to that chair. I wanted to move; my instinct was to get up. I felt vulnerable. I felt alone. Where the hell was Angelina when I needed her?

'Angelina?'

'Heather, be careful. This girl is not what she seems. I'm not sure who or what she is, but she is dark. She is still blocking me; I can't speak to her. She is a dark entity.'

'And the other one? The mother?'

'She's been shrouded all evening. I didn't feel her coming. She is dark.'

'Heather, do something! This isn't right!' Deni tugged at my finger. 'Heather, do something.'

'Come, Sarah, leave this woman and use me. She cannot cope with your presence. Use me as your channel; use my energy. You must use me.'

'Heather,' she spoke softly.

Hearing my name spoken by this entity was a little unnerving, Dawn's voice was high and light with an edge of sarcasm bleeding through it, or should I say Sarah's voice.

'Heather,' she repeated, almost playing with the word on her tongue as she played with the flame. 'Heather, is there light or dark in thy soul?'

I couldn't move my eyes from her face; something about the sound of her voice had me glued at this moment. I tried to speak and realised I couldn't. My mouth had dried up, my words lay somewhere between my ears.

'Heather, I ask again. Is there light or dark within thy soul?' Her lank hair again swayed as she moved from side to side, her stare still firm on my face. 'I fear thy soul be dark, Heather. Black as this night, as the sky falls around thy ears, taking thy heart in its palm and crushing with the might of thy elders. Thou sit in earnest, Heather, but thou have no understanding.'

With that, Dawn sat back in her chair, her hand withdrew from the flame and again lay flat and firm on the cloth. She closed her eyes. It was as if she were a mechanical wind-up toy whose spring had run out—bloody eerie.

'What's that smell? Can anyone else smell that?' Deni cried as she gripped Dawn's hand. 'Heather, do something. The smell's coming from her; it smells like burning, her hand is burning up.' Deni was screaming.

'Please, Deni, it's ok. I know you are afraid, but Dawn will be fine. Please, let us stay focused.' I was shaking in my seat, could feel the freezing temperature beginning to numb my legs. Here I was, trying to reassure Deni when I could smell it myself, an awful stench of burning.

I looked over at Maggie. Her eyes were still adamant on Dawn.

'Maggie?' I asked gently. I was worried about this poor woman. She'd hardly been lucid all evening, then to start rambling. 'Maggie, are you alright?'

She turned a slow-motion movement, which had my attention tethered between its creepy fingers. Her head shifted slowly; it tilted to one side. She was looking at me but was not looking at me at the same time. It was as if her eyes had glazed over. She smiled.

'Maggie, who is this Maggie? Ah…' she paused a second, 'this gentlewoman who sits at thy table. Who listens to the folly of this room, this mockery that suggests light?' Her voice was steady and calm, but I could sense her fingers gripping mine. Her strength was great; I wanted to wrench my hand free as she squeezed harder still. She raised her eyebrows.

'Light thou ask. Light has long since been diminished. The darkness of man and all that he does in the name of the Lord God,' she laughed. 'God? Who sits and watches as a child's life is being sucked from her skin, as the reaper stands watchman over her bed, watching and waiting to claim her soul, her poor delicate soul? Thy God does nothing.'

She blinked; her eyes stayed closed a second or two. Too long, she opened them upon me with a new knowing gaze. 'Heather, thou are but an instrument, thou are not aware of what thou do. The questions that must be answered. The wrongdoing that thee will answer for.' Maggie's hand released my finger, her palm flat, her fingers splayed upon the cloth, her face gestured towards the candle.

'My mother promised, swore to keep the child safe from the darkness that dwelled within my soul, that does dwell within my soul this very night. The darkness that would be her end.' Her head fell forward, her arms slack.

I was being played. I was getting pissed off! It was at that point I knew enough was enough. There was no way I was letting it get any further out of control.

'Heather, the woman has gone. I can only sense the child. She had dropped her cover. I think the other was the shroud. You need to get her out, take her to the light.'

Out the corner of my eye, I could see the curtains whipping violently against the window. The atmosphere deteriorated further; Deni was screaming hysterically now. I thought she was about to run out; I gripped her fingers tight to keep her there. It was one of those moments that you seem to observe from a distance, as though you are not there but are just a watcher.

I looked up to see Alex pacing the table with the thermal imager. I remember shouting at the top of my voice, loud over the hysteria.

'Sarah, you will leave this woman now! You must leave this atmosphere!' My words were lost as Dawn sat upright, her eyes opened and fixed upon my face. 'Sarah, you must leave this woman now!' I repeated my order, not something I was in the habit of doing. Have never really needed to do it.

It was at that moment, I felt as though hell was going to swallow us whole, dragged deep into the midst of where this soul seemed to be taking us.

Deni screeched as I turned back to Dawn. Her eyes stayed transfixed to mine again as her body thrashed from side to side. Oh shit.

'Burn and be burned. Thou shall all burn for the sins of Man.' I could hear this voice, but it was no longer coming from Dawn. I watched her face as Sarah repeated her words. 'Burn for the sins of Man.'

Dawn's body was swaying again, Maggie was motionless, as customary, and Deni was still weeping. All hands

91

remained in a circle. Again, I looked at each face in turn. Yet, I could still hear the words repeat, over and over. 'Burn and be burned.'

They were in my head; the bitch was in my head, screaming at the top of her voice.

'Get out of my head, Sarah,' I demanded through gritted teeth. I was shaking, trying not to lose the plot. 'Sarah, get out of my head now! You must leave this place at once, go into the light. You don't belong here now. Leave this house and be gone.' I was shouting now. I could feel the anger and fear bubble in my chest. I wanted to scream and lash out. 'Sarah, you must leave this place, now.'

Looking around the room, I wasn't sure what response I could gain, but I shouted at the women. 'Keep the circle tight, don't let it break. We must remain strong together.'

I took a deep breath, 'Be gone, spirit, be gone from this place.' I shouted with as much resolve as I could muster from my tattered nerves. I was shaking, my throat sore and hoarse. I couldn't see.

My world went black.

Chapter Sixteen

It was like I was somewhere else.

I wasn't there at all. As if watching a movie or peering through a frosty window. I could see myself and the other women sat around the table. Our hands clenched together in a circle on the cloth. The edges of which were rippled, as in movement, but static in the air like a camera shot. The curtains were also captured in a whipping motion. The room was dark but very still, the candle alight with a tall flame. It sat immobile and tranquil.

Everyone's eyes were tightly shut. The room was suspended in time, motionless. Alex stood planted behind me, still firmly gripping his EMF and thermal reader. I could hear a pounding in my ears, faint at first, then quickly getting louder and stronger. It wasn't my heartbeat but Alex's. I looked at his face, white as a sheet with huge fearful eyes.

Oh, his lovely big baby blues, I thought. One day, I shall tell him how much I love him.

With that, my body came crashing down, my head hit the table, hands both sides of me held on tight. I could feel a hand on my shoulder. I could hear a voice in my ear, this time not in my head.

'Heather, are you okay? Is it over? Has... has she gone?' Very slowly, my dazed head lifted to see Maggie leaning across to look at me. Her lovely face was tender and soft. Her eyes were gentle and knowing. 'Are you OK? Has she gone now?'

'Is everyone alright?' My eyes went to each in turn, all faces pale and shaken but coherent. 'Dawn?'

'I think I'm… fine.' She glanced around the room, first to her sister, then her mother. They both nodded. 'Yes, I'm alright. Heather?'

'I think…' I paused, sat back in my chair. Our hands were still clenched. I think they were too scared to let go. I looked over my shoulder at Alex, wanting somehow for him to give her the thumbs up; he just shrugged.

The candle wore a regular flame, no flicker of activity. The curtains that had been thrashing from the pole now hung calmly at peace at the window. Alex once again wandered the room with the EMF; his motion eased me as it always did.

'Readings are normal again; it only measures five milligauss. It had gone right up to fifteen.' Alex continued to patrol the room. 'I'll know more when I watch the camera footage back.'

'What happened?' Dawn looked at her mother and then at me. 'Heather?' Her face was ashen, but she seemed to remember nothing. Just as well, I thought.

'Heather, she hasn't gone.'

'What?'

'What's the matter, what's going on?' cried Deni.

'She is still here. Sarah, you must leave this house; you must go into the light. You must move on to the next world. You no longer belong here. You must leave,' I continued to recite.

'I don't understand. She's gone, hasn't she?' Deni continued crying.

'Spirit, you must leave this place; you no longer belong here. Go into the light, spirit.' My heart pounded inside my ribcage as I felt a cold hand around my neck. 'NOW, spirit, you must go into the light. Leave this place. You no longer belong… here in this world,' I gagged, gasping for breath.

My words were distorted as I could feel myself choking. I sat back on my chair with her spirit hand clutching my throat—tight.

The candle's flame flickered and then was gone. I mustered up all my psychic energies, along with Angelina's protection.

'SPIRIT, LEAVE THIS PLACE AND BE GONE!'

The drapes swung erratically at the window, whipping Deni in the back of her head. The table lurched back and forward under our hands. I urged everyone to focus and repeat with me.

'Spirit, leave this place and be gone! Spirit, leave this place and be gone!' Again, and again.

A series of loud bangs and crashes spread through the dining room; cupboard doors slapped violently on their hinges, china ornaments were propelled across the room and came crashing to the floor. The table rumbled with movement, it tipped from leg to leg, digging its hard edge into our stomachs, but still, we continued to chant.

All our eyes carried up toward the light fitting above our heads; it flashed on and then off again, periodically illuminating the dense darkness of the dining room. Over and over, the bulbs glowed before they made an incredible crackling spark and exploded, splattering the tablecloth with hard needles of broken glass.

Panicked screams penetrated the atmosphere.

Then, nothing.

The table came to an abrupt stop. The extinguished candle sat with its flame once more.

I sat back on the chair, my heart in my mouth, my throat gravelly and sore. Dawn sat facing, her eyes wide and bewildered, trembling in her seat.

'Has she gone now?'

'I think so.' I turned to Alex.

'The EMF reading is normal again,' he shrugged.

Alex opened the dining-room door, switching on the hall light. The room was a devastating sight. Broken china and glass ornaments lay shattered in a million pieces on the carpet. The curtains no longer draped the window but twisted and coiled the wooden pole, a tangled mess of blue fabric. A deep sigh of relief sounded from Dawn as she sat back, hands on her battered head.

'Well, I'll get this mess cleared up in the morning. You need some sleep.' Deni took Dawn's hand, helping her up. Both girls stood for a moment, cuddled in a mass of arms and matted hair. Deni wept on her shoulder. 'I thought I'd lost you there for a while. Bloody terrified me. I don't mind admitting it.'

Dawn looked at her sister, her face battered, a splattering of tiny cuts from the shattered ornaments. She wiped her hand over her sister's cheeks, smoothing out her hair.

Something inside my stomach lurched. I felt physically sick.

I sat back down on my chair, my head between my knees. My ears were ringing. My arms were heavy and tingled like the first moments of pins and needles when the sensation begins to return. I was shaking.

Alex knelt in front of me. I could feel his breath on my head wisp my hair, but I just couldn't look up. My brain was spinning inside my skull. A great whirling of red and orange sat behind my eyelids.

'Heth?'

I could hear his words, but they were so distant, like being spoken through a tube. I was there, but I wasn't. At that moment, I was nowhere. I didn't exist.

'Heather. Heather, go back. You need to go back.'

'Heth, please love, what's the matter.'

Alex was getting closer, I could hear him calling me, and I was running, sprinting. I needed to get to him. I was reaching out to him.

'Heth. Look at me.' He lifted my chin. I couldn't open my eyes. I wanted to.

'Heather. Stay with Alex.'

I opened my eyes with such a start it made me jump, along with Alex. His face was so close; I could see all those lovely little freckles that spattered his nose; his big blue eyes were dark and panic-stricken.

'What's the matter?' Alex's voice was low, as if not to worry the others in the room. I could see them all staring at me.

'I don't know what's wrong… maybe I'm coming down with something.'

'Yes, spirit-it is,' he smirked, but there was a serious undertone.

'Heather, I'm afraid to ask but, has she gone now? She has, hasn't she?' Deni stood behind Alex, her hands worrying at her mouth. 'Please say it's all over.'

I tried to smile as I called to Angelina. If ever I really needed her, it was now. I needed to know it was safe.

'She's gone, Heather.'

Chapter Seventeen

Alex heaved the gadgets into the car.

I stood on the doorstep, saying my goodbyes.

'I don't know how to thank you enough, Heather? But she was scary, wasn't she?' Dawn's pale features still quivered with torment.

'Yes, Dawn, I'm not sure if she was bad, so to speak, or just angry. If we pass over in bad or tragic circumstances, we can take all that fear and anger with us. And she was just a child; imagine that poor child when she was alive, afraid and in pain. But yeah, she was scary.'

'Get back in the door, now!'

I hesitated for a second, a second too long, as with a great bang, the heavy front door slammed. Shutting me out, but more ominously, locking Dawn and her family inside with, well, with something that was becoming extremely dangerous.

'Heather, she's still here. She's still inside the house. You need to get back in there now!'

The words sent shivers of fear through my body. I banged furiously at the door, but it wasn't budging. I could see the visible terror on the captive's faces.

'We can't open the door, Heather! What's going on?' The faint cry seeped through the letterbox into the night air.

Alex grabbed the wheel brace from the boot, ramming the plain edge between the door and the frame.

'Mind out the way!' I shouted as loudly as possible in the hope of being heard over the frenzied howling inside.

After a massive thrust and a yank with the metal instrument, the frame gave way, splintering the wood surrounding the Yale lock. The door opened into the hallway as an eerie silence fell on the house. Silence, however, is never a good sign, not in these circumstances. Both Dawn's mother and sister stood in utter bewilderment, their faces drenched in terror.

'Where's Dawn?'

'In there,' her mother gestured to the dining room.

An odd sound of screeching and wailing; the young woman with lank hair and pallid skin lay crunched on the floor in the corner of the room. The dining room was still in darkness with only the luminosity from the hallway, but I could see the outline impression of someone behind her; a child, a young girl, maybe no more than nine or ten. Hair that in life had been dark now appeared incandescent. But her almost black eyes stared at me, dagger-sharp.

'Dawn, Dawn, can you hear me?' Tentatively, I stood on the threshold, neither in nor out of the room. There came no reply, only the wailing; her weary body lurched back and forth in a rocking motion. The spirit of Sarah stood watching, eyes bold and wicked, her translucent arm outstretched, her hand poised above Dawn's head as if a demonic puppeteer.

'You no longer belong here, Sarah. It is time you were on your way. Leave her.' Desperately, I attempted reasoning with what seemed a non-respondent entity, then I heard a weak voice from behind me.

'Heather, I don't understand what's going on. Is that a girl in there with her? I heard her voice screaming through the air, and then the front door slammed.'

'What did you hear? Did she say anything?'

'Just a lot of nonsense, I couldn't make anything out, but she did keep…' she hesitated; the strangeness of what she'd heard baffled her. 'She said the General, the General, over and over.'

'Yes, I know… I didn't see it earlier, but I understand now.'

'Understand what? I don't understand any of this. Why is this happening to us?'

'I think she was burned… Sarah, she was a witch. Or rather she was…'

'Heather, there's no time to explain. She's becoming stronger.'

I coiled round to observe the spirit. No words leaked from her foul mouth, but I could hear her all the same. Her loud and strangely distorted muttering. She was now chanting.

'Heather, it's some sort of chant or curse.'

I had never, until that moment, encountered anything that was so adamant, so obstinate.

'She won't listen to me. You need to get Dawn out of there before it's too late.'

'Sarah!' I shouted. 'You cannot hold Dawn and her family responsible for what happened.'

She continued to chant her curse, simply smiling as she did so. Evil seemed to ooze from each unearthly pore of her spirit body. Sarah removed her glare from mine and returned it to Dawn's slumped figure. Tilting her head to gaze upon her prey, again, she raised her hand, reeling Dawn's torso back and forth, her limp hair swinging with the velocity of her movement.

'Heather, now. You need to get Dawn out of there before it's too late.'

I only had a few moments.

I relit the large candle placing it back on the dining table, constantly keeping my psychic eye on Sarah. Dawn's body lay immobilised, slumped over her knees. Sarah watched me almost in amusement and delight at my attempt to challenge her. But I stood poised and ready. My heart beating in my ears, my eyes fixed on the spirit presence.

'Angelina, I need your help now like no other time. I am afraid more so than ever before.'

'Heather, I have always been by your side, guiding and protecting you. Now is no different. You are strong, stronger than even you can imagine.'

My last resort, I had no choice. I stood tall. My eyes were wide. My demeanour was faithful and constant. Although inside, my nerves were frayed, and my body trembled. My last resort. This was always my last option. If this didn't work, I was coming back with a priest.

With spirit protection and guidance, I started to conduct the prayer, a Latin prayer or exorcism if you like, the exorcism of Sarah, to send her on to where she belonged.

'Exorcizo te, omnis spiritus immunde, in nomine Dei…' I could hear cries from the hallway as Dawn's body lifted slightly, 'Patris omnipotentis, et in noimine Jesu.' I continued, 'Christi Filii ejus, Domini et Judicis nostri, et in virtute Spiritus…'

The moments stretched, seconds became minutes, and I repeated the prayer, steadfast and true. Loud cries and piercing shrieks shelled the air drowning out the whimpers of angst and panic that drifted from the dark hallway. The only light visible was the flickering flame, pure and strong, and the dim light from the streetlamp through the ragged curtains.

Sarah's spirit lifted her arms, and with an exaggerated sweep, Dawn's body was flung across the floor. She lay limp on the dark carpet. Her eyes closed, her breathing swift and shallow. I saw her mother tense. Her instinct to run and protect her child. I quickly held up my hand, a gesture of 'no leave her'.

I could see the danger in Sarah's eyes, a glint of a smirk 'two for the price of one'. Maggie stopped mid-motion at the threshold.

My voice, loud and strong, I continued reciting the Latin words, again and again. I could feel a hand on my shoulder, the tender touch of guiding spirit, her words echoing and mirroring mine.

Within a flicker of the candle, the entity evaporated from my psychic perception, leaving the room cold and empty.

Instantaneously, a wild gust and a piercing wailing lashed the room. Debris from the séance whipped into the air. Dawn's limbs stretched and tangled in her silent, relentless torture. The invisible hostile arms thrashed the furniture, chairs, cupboard doors, curtains.

'Exorcizo te, omnis spiritus immunde, in nomine Dei …Patris omnipotentis,' I shouted.

The highest pitched sound, an unimaginable cry of pain and anger, throttled the air, trembling, shattering every molecule of the surroundings. I turned to see the others, their hands over their ears, desperate to block the deafening shrieks—Whirlwind, turmoil, and tremors. I could feel her spirit heaving and retching with resistance. It was only a matter of time; she wouldn't be able to hold on much longer—surely.

The windowpanes rattled inside their frames as she wailed with one last effort of battle.

The dining table tipped and tilted, knocking my hip as I stumbled; I lost my footing. The white candle rapidly slipped along the polished surface, landing on the carpet, a mess of hot wax and a thin whisper of grey vapour from the extinguished flame.

Silent, still, and frozen.

No one moved; only our eyes wandered the devastation and debris, timidly searching. Exhausted and numb with cold, I tentatively approached Dawn. Her body lay still.

'Dawn?'

She came to, her entire body shaking, aching with pain. Purple bruises and inflamed carpet burns covered her arms and knees. Within an instant, Maggie and Deni were there, holding and stroking her hair, cold and wet with sweat.

Tentatively, I watched Dawn quietly observed her movements, her expression. She seemed back to herself. My nerves kept me static for a few more moments.

I didn't dare hope now. Sarah had been so cunning.

'Angelina?'

'It's safe. I can no longer feel or sense her. She was tough. I mean strong. There was no way she was letting me close. She kept laughing at me. But it's now safe.'

Fuck, I needed a brandy.

Chapter Eighteen

Early hours

The street is how we left it.

Only a few down funnels of yellow lamplight the length of the street, the silhouetted houses being swallowed by the night behind.

It's too quiet.

Alex pulls up in the same parking spot directly outside. I gaze up at the house. Okay, I need to get out of this bloody car. I feel bonded to my seat.

'Come on.' Alex is taking the lead. I know I should be more on it, but that feeling is still burrowing its way into my chest.

'Okay, let's do this.' My outward bravado is winning. Alex smiles and squeezes my thigh. He winks and opens his door. I follow suit.

The house is silent. I've imagined all sorts of awful scenarios on our way. But honestly, if I didn't know better, I would assume everyone to be in bed asleep. I push on the splintered front door. The lock is useless and broken. The darkness hits me, the same depth of solid oblivion that I've had to deal with the whole journey back. I step over the threshold. I can feel Alex directly behind me, his breath welcome as it ruffles the top of my head.

'Please, stay close to me,' I plead.

'I'm here.' His hand sits on my shoulder.

We are in the front hall.

'Dawn?' I call. 'Deni?' No answer. 'It's Heather. We're here; where are you?'

I stand static for a minute or two, waiting, hoping for a reply.

Nothing.

I scan my hand over the wall to find the switch; it's here somewhere. I find it, click, nothing! The lights are out—Fab! I look over into the dining room, nothing. I want to look around behind the door to check but just can't bring myself to go in there. Alex steps in front of me; his hand strokes my cheek, it lingers. He knows I'm scared; he won't say so, though. He wanders in. Again, he tries the light switch—no joy. Broken fragments crunching beneath his soles, I jump, then he bashes into a fallen chair. He does a three-sixty—nothing.

'Maybe the kitchen…' I suggest with a squeak.

We hear a voice, low and hushed, no more than a muffle.

Alex takes my hand as we pace towards the open door. He pointlessly tries the kitchen light. The kitchen's darkness is eerily punctuated by the odd red LED light; the microwave, dishwasher, the oven clock is flashing. This helps give us some bearings. My eyes scan the huge room. I feel a bar stool bump my leg. I'm further in than I thought. I spin around to find Alex; I sense him sigh as he pats my arm. I turn toward the pantry where Maggie had stood earlier. I can hear the muttering again. Alex is there before I can even move my feet. He's fumbling for the handle; he's cursing under his breath as we hear weeping coming from behind the door.

'Quick Heth, help me open this effing door.' He's tugging at the handle. It's a round brass knob, no grip and keeps sliding out of his hand. 'Effing thing!' The words are whispered, but he's losing it now.

'It's okay, we can do this. It's just a bloody knob.'

I grip the round handle with both hands, managing to twist it slowly. The door is stiff and wedged somewhere at the top. I can feel it relenting; with a swift jerk, it flings open, hitting my brow bone.

'Fuck it!' I swear as my hand explores the lump already swelling beneath my fingertips.

'Heather…' my name is slow on Alex's lips. 'There's no one in here.'

He fumbles around and click—a God-sent light. It's one of those battery push lights; I've never been so thankful for such a mundane gadget. It barely glows, the batteries need changing, but it's enough to see the space. Old paper-covered shelves, veg, tins, and a few stacked boxes. But it's empty.

'What the… I know what I heard. Heather, you heard it too, didn't you?'

I just nod, wide-eyed.

I turn quickly. Something has just moved in the kitchen. It's near the microwave, no more than a few feet away. I can still feel the residue movement like a wisp of air across my face.

Someone's calling me. I'm not sure if it's real or psychically. It's hard to tell. The voice is stifled, almost—the same weeping from the empty pantry. I gazed quizzically at Alex within the ever-fading light. His face is intense.

'Did you hear that again? Or is it in my bloody head?'

'No, I heard it, but there's something odd about it… something I can't put my finger on.' His hands are squeezing my shoulders. 'Effing hell Heather, I knew this was all bloody wrong!' He's angrily shaking his head.

'I think it's coming from upstairs. It sounds like Deni,' I whisper, scanning the room before me. 'I'm not actually sure. She sounded odd on the phone like it was more than just fear. Alex, look at me.' I'm trying to take control. 'None of that matters now; we just need to find everyone, make sure they're ok.'

It's nearly dark now. The batteries have had it; the light is giving up the ghost. We are in total darkness again. Deeper now as our eyes are scrambling to adjust.

'You stay down here. I'm going upstairs.' Alex is already heading for the kitchen door. He's no longer in arms reach. 'Stay down here, have another look in the dining room.'

Okay, time to get my shit together. For heaven's sake, Heather, you are a professional; this is your job, your calling, this is your life. But I know as I'm giving myself a bloody good talking to, I'm suffocating with an awful feeling of dread. I can feel spirit hands around my throat. I'm in danger. And where the bloody hell is Angelina when I need her? I've been calling her since we pulled up.

Then, it hits me. It's that precise thought that's at the root of this fear. After all, she's been with me since I was six, and nearly thirty years later, I can't remember a day when she hasn't been with me. This is why I'm feeling so in danger. It's my soul that's at risk here, and she is the one who always stands guard on the other side.

'Angelina, please. I need to know what's going on.'

I hear a thud from upstairs. It's loud and reverberates through the ceiling above my head.

'Alex?' I shout but don't as my throat is constricted. His name leaves my mouth in a pathetic whisper. 'Alex?' I try again with solid determination.

'I'm fine.' His hushed words escape through the floorboards above me.

'Any joy?' I call, but no answer. I hesitate for a second; should I follow him up?

'Stay down there.' His voice is more muffled now; I can't make out where it's coming from. But I do as I'm told.

Maybe I should recheck the front rooms. But I worry about Alex. He's doing the 'man thing'. But he has no defence against a spirit. I can't be angry. This is so unlike me to be so stupid—so scared.

I haven't moved from the spot; I'm still standing in the pantry doorway. My feet are solid beneath me as if fear has poured cement down my legs. They feel heavy as I walk towards the central island. If I can get there, I can navigate the room.

'Heather.'

Thank heavens, Angelina—about bloody time.

'Angelina, thank God. I need you. I can't seem to get myself together.'

No answer.

'Angelina, is she still here? Is Sarah still blocking you?'

I hold onto the back of a barstool; my eyes have adjusted enough to grasp the kitchen's layout. This was the stool I sat at earlier, Alex to my right, the girls opposite, and Maggie on the end to my left. My eyes move from seat to seat, gathering my thoughts of the evening. There's a movement. It's coming from the pantry where I was just standing. It's slow. Not a dash. I can't quite make it out. I look around the kitchen again; there's the dishwasher light and the microwave standby glowing orange. But as my eyes move, I can no longer see the flashing cooker digits—they're gone. Off? No, someone's standing in front of them.

'Heather.'

'Angelina?'

'Heather.'

'Angelina?'

No, this isn't my guide. The voice is in my head, but it's not her. Bitch!

'Oh, Heather, why are thou so afraid? Thy fear pours like water from a jug. I can almost taste it upon my tongue. It is sweet. Come, sit with me a while.'

'Where's Angelina? What do you want?'

'Oh, thou are so impatient. Dearest Angelina is taking a little rest; she has been so bothersome. Pestering, like a child fussing at my skirts.'

'What have you done to her? What the hell can you do to her?'

I'm now panicking.

'Oh, do hush. She will be well. She is of no interest to me. Heather, I have waited a long time for thee.'

The voice is now louder between my ears. Silky and enticing. I'm still staring at the cooker but realise the clock is now flashing—bold red digits. She's moved. My head nearly spins off my shoulders.

Someone, a figure, a woman, is sitting opposite me now. I can see her silhouette, dimly outlined. The door slams violently behind me. What light there was from the street outside is gone.

I'm frozen, stuck here in the kitchen in the dark with some psycho spirit.

'So, what do you want, Sarah? You don't belong here anymore. You need to leave this house, leave these poor women alone.'

I'm slowly gathering feeling in my legs. But I'm hot, burning up. I'm feeling unwell.

I want to sit down, but that's what she wants.

My instincts are to run.

I need to find the others.

I need to find Alex. I know he's only upstairs. I just need to get through the door.

Why can't I move?

Just take a step.

But I can't. She has me pinned. At this very moment, I feel so completely alone.

'Oh, Heather, thou are so foolish.'

Her voice is hypnotic inside my brain. I want her out.

'What do you want? I can help you go into the light. I can help you rest in peace. You will be with family and loved ones.'

'There is no light, foolish woman.'

She's getting under my skin. I know it's a game.

'I was nicely asleep in my bed, and you dragged me over here again. So, what is it? What the hell do you want with these girls, with Dawn? Why are you still here?'

I'm getting pissed off.

She's laughing. Her voice is soft. Despite my longing to run, I find myself pulling out the barstool. My hands are gripping the cool chrome frame.

I'm wondering what the hell I'm doing.

I resist, but I sit down hard upon the padded seat. The stool pushes in, loudly scraping along the floor tiles with a nerve-wrenching screech. The marble edge of the island digs into my stomach as I'm wedged under. Restricted, my feet jammed between chrome and wooden legs.

'Now, Heather, is that not better. There be no need to stand; I feel we should be better acquainted.'

'No, I don't think we should; I think I've had just about enough of you tonight.'

'Oh, but Heather, we have only just begun.'

'Sarah, just tell me why you're here? I can help you move to the light. You no longer belong here; you're dead.'

I'm desperate to claim this situation. There is one rule in my life—stay in control. That whole sentiment seems to have gone straight out the bloody window tonight.

I lay my hands flat on the marble surface, eyes directly focused on the silhouetted figure across from me. I can't make out who it is. Is it one of the women? Of course, it is! I'm talking to the spirit, but the body it is possessing is as real as I am. Rationally thinking, I'd assume it was Dawn. But there is something in the way this woman is sitting. Not that I can tell, they all have long hair and are about the same stature. This is where Angelina would be of help.

Now I'm thinking of her, what this entity has done to her. And where is Alex? I'm willing him to come back down. If he hasn't found the other two upstairs, why hasn't he come down?

'Sarah. What have you done to Alex?' I say this aloud; my mind has had enough. This bitch has just about ruined my night. I'm now pissed off. 'Sarah, you will answer me, and you will leave this place, and if you don't want to go into the light, go the fuck back to where you come from.'

The figure shuffles on the stool; I can only hear it. The darkness is too distorting. My eyes are starting to play tricks. The more I concentrate, the worse it gets. I want to close my eyes.

Then, I feel fingertips touch mine. Just the tips, very slightly. I jump, goosebumps scurry down my back. A voice, gentle and tender. It's getting closer. She is singing, no, chanting. It's so low I can't make it out. My ears are buzzing with the silence.

'Oh, Heather. Oh, the folly of your own belief. Thou are a greater fool than I thought thou would be.'

Her clear words coil in the air between us. It's no longer whispered in the darkness of my mind. She is speaking across from me. I can feel the lingering threads of the syllables on my face as the words leave her lips—sticky and deadly sweet, like tainted honey. The woman is moving. Her face is coming closer. I want—need, to back away, but the stool is rigid behind my body.

I'm trapped.

Her face is before me now. My eyes can't quite make out her features, but I feel the essence of her face imprinted behind my eyes. I see her in my mind rather than with my stare.

'There be no light. There be only darkness.'

Her hand whips up from the table. She's quick. Her palm is cold.

I'm frozen.

I can't move.

My hands are stuck to the marble. She touches my cheek, trailing her fingers across my face. I wince as they skim my brow. They're soft and gentle as they move down to my neck.

With a speed that draws every ounce of breath from my lungs, she grips my throat.

I think I'm choking, but I'm not—I can't. I have no air or movement to choke or splutter. I want to struggle. I want to fight. I want to, but I can't.

I'm paralysed.

She is strong.

I am now drifting.

It's dark, I'm cold. So very cold.

'Thou are such a fool. I am not Sarah. I am thy undoing.'

Chapter Nineteen

Swiftly, Alex makes it to the kitchen door.

A shard of eerie green light glows through the front door's stained-glass panel. The staircase is to his right. His foot finds the bottom step. Climbing two at a time, he moves quickly as the staircase bears round. The thump in his ribcage is heavy in his ears. The house is unnaturally silent. There is no light on the upstairs landing, just doors.

There it is again—a whimper.

It's one of the girls, yes it must be, and maybe she's hurt? He needs to find her.

He's had enough of this. He doesn't do the 'spirit' thing; he's an academic, he can always find the rationale. It's what he does. His thoughts dash to Heather. He's worried about her. She believes in what she does, her talents, her gift, her guide. Alex believes in her, even if he doesn't believe in spirits. There is something wrong with the whole investigation. Alarm bells have rung since he took the call from Denise. He couldn't put his finger on it. It seemed legit enough. And so, he stifled his doubts. He wishes he'd told Heather then, he wishs they'd never taken the case.

He needs to find the women and get back to Heather, then get out of this house.

Alex takes small steps along the hallway, listening at the doors. He lightly pats his way along the surface to find a handle. Cold metal, round, a doorknob, he turns it, slowly it opens. He faces the opening as warm air, the smell, a combination of fabric softener and musty oldness slaps his face—the airing cupboard.

Alex fumbles in his back pocket. Why hadn't he thought of this earlier? He pulls his mobile phone out of his jeans and swipes his thumb across the screen. A stark white light hits his face, harsh as his eyes adjust. The limited light is enough to see the hallway is narrow and that the far door at the end is ajar. He takes a step, stubbing his toe on the open door.

'Bloody hell!' He curses as he kicks the door to.

'Alex?' It's Heather.

'I'm fine,' he answers in a soft call, almost trying not to disturb the house.

'Any joy?' she calls again. Alex fiddles with his phone as it blacks out. He swipes his thumb again, the phone almost slipping through his fingers. After a moment of an impromptu juggle, he gathers a firm grip.

'Stay down there,' he calls through his hand. There's an awful sensation of being watched. No, it's more than that. It's as if there are eyes, faces in the darkness, as if it's made of something tangible. He shivers.

That's enough of that crap, Alex; pull yourself together.

Alex is standing in the bedroom doorway now. His feet have pulled him towards it. The dimness of the outside streetlight gives the bedroom a sinister quality. He hovers in the threshold. He can just make out the line of the wardrobe, the chest of drawers under the window. The bed is the dominating shape. He takes a couple of steps until the mattress nudges at his knees.

A movement. A breeze. A sound—the whimper.

Alex holds his phone out at arm's length, scanning it around the room, trying to find the source. There's a huddled figure, crouched in the corner between the wall and bedside table. It's one of them, which one he cannot see. Her hair is long and dark, her head down beneath her arms as she clutches her knees. She's shaking, rocking.

'Dawn?' Alex is desperate to keep his voice calm, but it quakes with an unusually high-pitched tone. 'Dawn?' He calls again, this time with a little more conviction. 'Bloody hell, are you alright?'

Alex wants to turn and leave the room, stay where he is at the very least, but his conscience takes him around the other side of the room. He kneels in front of the weeping girl.

There's a loud screeching, a scraping, coming up through the floorboards, his desperate mind switches to Heather.

'Dawn, we must get up; we have to get out.'

Shoving his phone back in his jeans, he's scrambling to find her hands. She's a mass of interwoven limbs.

'Dawn, look up.' He's assuming it's her; the shaking mass is dressed in pyjamas; he has no idea. It could be Deni. 'Where is your sister, your mother?' He's eager to sound calm, reassuring at best. Inside he is a web of jangling nerves. 'What's happened?'

Dawn looks up from under her mass of tangled hair, her cheeks pale and ghostly in the dim light. The curtains are open, the streetlight makes her face almost glow. She is staring now—wide, saucer eyes of fear.

'There be no light for me, only darkness.'

'God, I know. What happened? I had no idea where your trip switch was, and there just hasn't been time…' he hesitates. 'Dawn?'

'Have I not told thee?' She wipes her face on her arm, nudging the hair from her brow. 'There be only darkness this night.'

'Sarah?' Alex slumps back on his heels, staring at the girl.

'I was always searching for the light. I did not want to go with the shadows…' she sighs with a suppressed cry as she shakes. 'But alas, they took me. The candle…' she leans forward. 'The candle, always be sure to leave a candle burning,' she sighs again. 'Evil lurks behind the darkness.'

Alex just stares, with no real idea what to do but get out.

Dawn stares back. Her large eyes blink with an essence of simplicity.

'I resisted 'til my body ached, and my heart stung, my soul was pulled into the shadows. And then…' tears again, she is wailing, a high-pitched childlike scream. 'And then I was gone. Dead.'

'Sarah.'

What should he say? What can he say to that? There's a conscious truth and innocence about her words. Her voice, light and clear. This isn't like the usual ramblings of a disembodied spirit. He can feel the rhythm of his beating heart, thunderous in his ears.

What would Heather do?

Oh my God, Heather.

'Sarah, we must get downstairs. Heather, she is downstairs, she can help you. We can help you,' he nods, enticing her to stand.

Alex tugs on her arms. Finding her hands, he pulls the girl to her feet. She sways on the spot, her hands gripping his. She's shuddering. Alex can feel every bone in her body tense. Her eyes wide and round—staring. She now stands rigid. Her head darts around. Her eyes blinking quickly, adjusting to the darkness. She gazes for a moment before she takes a pace quickly toward Alex, her movement's jerky.

'Alex?' her head spins around, searching the room, her fingernails gripping into his hands.

'Dawn?'

'Yes,' she answers quickly, her voice hushed. 'Alex, please help me.'

'Oh my God! Dawn. Sarah? What?'

'We need to get out now before they come back.'

'Who comes back, Dawn? You mean Sarah?'

'All of them.' Wide-eyed, like a feral cat caught in

headlights, she stands transfixed by fear. 'All of them.' Her voice breaks into a million particles as it hits his ears, splintering anything logical that has dwelt within his scientific brain. This is not real. This, and every other moment tonight, has not been real.

'Okay, downstairs now, let's get Heather and get out of here. Where are Deni and Maggie?'

'They...' she leans in close, her hair touches his face, her breath on his ear. 'They want something.'

The room is reeling, his world has lost all bearing, and all he can think of is Heather. Is it her they want? Alex drags Dawn around the bed, bashing his hip on the chest of drawers as he goes. It wobbles as something topples over. There's a moment's silence. He stops. His heart almost falters in his chest.

'Dawn, we need to be quick. What the hell do they... whoever they are, want with Heather?'

He's panicking now. Dawn doesn't answer. His arm is very nearly pulled from its socket. His hand is just on the edge of the bedroom door, his fingertips skimming the wood, but he is going nowhere.

'Why in such a hurry?'

The hand that holds his tightens; she pulls him back towards the bed. She is strong.

'There be no need for hurry, this night. Let us sit... play with me a while.'

'Sarah! Oh crap. Sarah, please, look, we don't have time for this. And we certainly don't have time to play games. How about we both go downstairs? Heather is downstairs; let's go see her, eh?'

Reluctantly, Alex sits down hard upon the bed, his hands in his lap. He looks down at them, wondering what the hell he is doing. He has no control whatsoever. No matter how much he tries, he can't move a digit. His fingers are tightly woven together. He can't resist her. She's playing with him.

'Now, is that not better.' It's a statement. Her hand strokes her hair, patting it down, smoothing it around her face. She wipes her tears from her cheeks with the back of her hand, wiping it across her runny nose.

'Sarah, we don't have time for this.'

'Oh, but we do. I have all of time. I have nothing but time.'

'We need to get to Heather. She can help you find your way,' Alex's voice is strained. He can hear his fear in every word, each syllable, a crumbling piece of his world disintegrating at his feet.

'Tell me a story? Or shall I indeed tell thee one?' She smiles as she looks toward the door.

Alex wants to turn to see whatever she sees; as her eyes widen, his head is fixed on his shoulders. He strains to move. He is as useless as a mannequin.

There are footsteps, soft and precise.

One. Two. Three.

They have stopped. He can hear breathing. It's close and warm on his cheek. A hand brushes a wave of hair from his ear. His eyes are fixed on Dawn's face as she smiles past him.

'There be no time for this.' The voice is low, hushed, whispering in his ear. 'Enticing as thou are,' she licks his cheek, her tongue coiling to his ear. He wants to vomit, but the sensation is more than fear or disgust. 'Very enticing, I can see why she is enamoured by thee. Oh, the games we could play. I would have such fun toying with thee. Thy skin is sweet like thy fear. Why do all men fear me so?' She laughs and kisses his cheek. 'Alas, it cannot be so.'

Then thud.

His world spins. He's falling. The bed is soft beneath him. It catches and cradles his head. He's weightless. It's pitch black now. The darkness is behind his eyes. He wants to sleep.

His legs are a twist beneath his weight. They ache, and so does his head.

Alex tries to wriggle, the space is black around him, and the air is thin and close—warm.

His arms are folded bizarrely beneath him, his cheek is pressed hard against the wooden floor. He can smell dust, musty and old. Something tickles his nose as he breathes, short and shallow—cobwebs. He needs to move; his weight is crushing his chest, but it's cramped, and he's stuck. He wriggles to free an arm, pushing himself up onto his elbow and bashes his head. The cupboard. He remembers opening a door only to find the airing cupboard.

The darkness is still spinning. He's trying to recall—how and why?

Heather, he needs to find her.

Dawn. Oh, he now remembers the words. The inner struggle. The beautiful voice. The whack to his skull. Hell!

Tentatively, he rubs the back of his head—a lump beneath his wet matted hair and a knotted mass of fresh and congealed blood.

The door opens with a sharp budge from his hips, he manages to crouch, but the space is small. At last, he rolls out into the hall. His brain feels as if it's split in two.

Scrambling to his feet, he heads to the stairs. His feet find them before his mind has time to register. An instant thought of taking them two at a time is short-lived as he trips. His body lurches forward, tumbling, hitting his shoulder on the corner of the staircase on the way down. He's a heap on the floor—a twisted mass at the foot of the stairs.

'Shit!'

The pain in his knee is almost unbearable as he tries to stand. His head spins in his hands. He rests against the wall.

The kitchen, he needs to get to the kitchen. He lunges at

the door. It's shut fast. He grabs the handle, twisting it. He's propelled inside as it gives way under his weight. He crashes into a bar stool. Quickly gathering his bearings, he pulls his phone from his back pocket and swipes the cracked screen. He scans the room. He turns a full circle.

There are noises, movements, whispers, a voice to his left, to his right. His head darts to find the source. She is chanting, singing, something soft and wistful.

Another voice, and another. A face is close to his now. Alex points the phone screen directly in front of him; across the island sits Dawn. Beside her, the others.

'Pleased thou could join us. Please, sit down.'

Unwillingly, Alex sits heavily upon the stool. The face in front still illuminated by his phone. He cannot move his eyes.

'That is better. This will never do; I do not like this contraption. A candle will be best.'

His phone screen dies, his eyes are searching blindly as an unseen hand strikes a match. Heather's half spent pillar candle flickers to life before him. The kitchen is aglow with a soft white light. The voice again, as he looks up, he sees Deni's face, soft and pretty. There is an essence of unrest behind her eyes, an inner struggle. The same underlying expression he saw in Dawn. His eyes dart around. Dawn and Maggie sit on either side of her.

His eyes search the kitchen.

'Where is Heather? What have you done to Heather?' Panicking now, his heart in his throat. 'Tell me where she is? If you have hurt her… I'll.'

'What would thou do? Kill me?' She softly laughs, 'Now, there be no need for that. I think I should tell thee a story.'

'Where is Heather?'

'Hush, boy.'

And with that, something covers his mouth, the impression of a hand. It smells of smoke.

Chapter Twenty

'There be no peace for thee, Master Hopkins.'

Manningtree - Samhain 1646

The candle was fading, short now, as were the remains of this night.

'Grandmother, please. I beseech thee, I need to understand. For I fear if I do not, then what chance will I have against the coming darkness.' The girl child looked towards the corner; they were restless, she could tell. They were there still, even with the approach of dawn. Would they fade? Or would they linger 'til the last? 'Thou know they come for me, Grandmother.'

The crone once again squeezed the child's hands. They were tiny, so fragile. She gently rubbed her arm. How could she let them take her? How could she save her from those beyond? They were coming this night as they had done so for the girl's mother. She had no way of stopping them or even halting them in their path; it was not in her power. As the night had progressed, so had the realisation. She knew the outcome of this night. As dawn would rise and touch the cottage thatch, so would the finality of existence—both the child's and her own.

'Morning broke, and they came with thick mud upon their boots. She knew they would come. She had held them off as long as she could,' the old woman sighed; the words she had kept hidden, silent, were bursting from her lips. No matter how she strived to keep them hushed, the time had come to tell. 'I promised thy mother I would never tell thee.' Her eyes closed, holding back tears.

'Grandmother.' The girl's tiny fingers caressed those old hands, '…please, do not weep, for I know what will be this day. I need only to settle my mind with the knowledge of the past.'

'I fear, child of mine own child, that I can no longer hold them back; they will come.' Those tears now fell. She took a deep breath, settling her mind to her task.

It would soon be over. She gazed into the child's eyes; they were dimming now. The light was fading. She had little time.

'She went willingly. We had hidden thee beneath, safe.' She glanced at the candle, an inch left, maybe if she was lucky. 'They asked of thee, they asked over and over. 'Dead,' she told them, 'Dead from fever,' so they searched, but they did not find thee, of course.' She touched her tiny cheek, moist beneath her old fingertips. 'I remained here in the cottage. They did not want me. They had come for thy mother, and only thy mother, and they accepted that thou had perished from fever. That fever had taken many a child, some even of those men that had come that morning. I saw the pain in their eyes.'

The girl concentrated hard on her grandmother's words.

'Why did they want my mother? Had she not helped, had she not helped those children, as she had helped me?' Her words were, of course, true.

'There are folk here in our own parish and beyond who do not like nor understand our ways. Our life has become a dangerous one. We have always helped those in need. Thou know thy mother was a cunning woman, a healer, has aided many to bear their children, healed both men and women in our own town with remedies. Thou understand what we have always done, what I still do?' She paused, 'although now, I do so in secret. Thou understand what we are, child?'

The girl pondered a moment. 'Of course, we are healers, cunning folk, which those men are afraid of. I hear them say we do the devil's work. Is that true, Grandmother?' Her wet eyes searched her grandmother's face, pleading.

'Of course, we do not. We only use the land, herbs, and Mother Nature herself to aid and heal; we are all daughters of the oak. Those that do cast such accusations only do so in fear, superstition, and stupidity. They fear God, and they fear and revere him,' she spat the word with a heart full of spite and hatred. For she had hated no man in her old life, but as she sat with the night passing like salt betwixt her fingers, her heart was full of nothing but abhorrence for that man. And she feared it.

'Thy mother had done something which I had begged her not to. It was this that had been her undoing.'

The girl sat in silence for a moment. She wanted to speak; her words sat heavy in her mouth, wanting to leap from her lips. She knew what her grandmother was speaking of.

'The darkness, Grandmother?'

'Yes, child, the darkness.'

'Why? I fear it. I fear it is not good, and no good will come of it, or me.'

Inside her chest, the crone's heart wept. The innocence and knowing of this child would soon be lost.

'Yes, child, but…' She paused, not sure how to continue. She reached for the small cup, placing the cool pottery to her lips. The tepid water lingered on her tongue for a moment. Replacing the cup, she shuffled closer. 'Darkness, thy mother felt was her only chance of saving thee.'

'Why would she?'

'She had done everything in her power, with herbs and remedies to save thee. Death was our lodger, sitting with us, waiting to take thee. Thou understand that many children had died. She had tried to save them. But they had died, nevertheless. The parents of those who perished blamed her. Their grief so torturous they needed someone to blame. There were rumours, gossip was spreading through the town that she was a…' she could not bring herself to say the word.

'Witch? I have heard it shouted and spat.'

'Oh, child, thy mother turned to the darkness to save thee. I could not stop her. She was strong, both of mind and resolve. She loved thee beyond any thought of consequence. But, of course, that consequence…' she left the rest unsaid. 'Her pact with the dark side had taken its toll on her. She became darkness herself. The word Witch was spoken again and again by the very folk she had helped. Finally, he had been summoned.'

'Who, Grandmother?'

'The man, Master Hopkins. Who was once the boy Matthew that she knew. His own fear of what he cannot explain, nor wants to, has brought his own kind of darkness upon his soul. For as a man, he has a dark and bitter heart.'

†

Her little legs scurried, her feet pushing her body as far up the bed as possible. She sat huddled against the headboard. But no matter how much she resisted, she knew this was what her poor heart had dreaded. Those dark, crawling fingers were gaining on her. They tugged at the bedclothes. They were swarming the floor now. A great, swirling mist of murky darkness was swallowing her bed. It carried great howling screams of lost souls. It carried her name. They screamed her name.

Then her mother's voice in her head.

'Sarah, my child.'

Her little hands covered her ears, tugging at her hair, pulling knotted chunks from her scalp as pain shredded her head in two. Her screams filled the cool air, her skin slick with sweat, her thin linen slip clinging to her frail body.

The crone watched.

The cold morning was gaining on them. Dawn was a matter of minutes away. The old woman stood with her back to the window. She could hear the boots of fearful men, with hatred and terror in their hearts and sticks and clubs in their hands. Although she could feel them gaining, closing the distance, she ignored them. She would deal with them soon enough.

She was powerless. She watched the consequence of her daughter's actions, now being claimed.

For there had been a condition.

'Help me, Grandmother.'

The crone remained motionless at the window.

'Help, please, I beg of thee.'

Her weary eyes wept as darkness claimed the child.

'Grandmother?'

'I cannot help thee, child. Thy mother's actions were her folly, and thou are paying for them. But, hush child, it will pass soon enough. Her meddling has claimed thou both to darkness. No good ever came of dark magic.'

The candle flickered its last as the flame fizzled and darkness befell the room.

On that cue, they leapt. The lost. The shadows. The evil. The wagers and bargains made by helpless souls. They all leapt at the poor child. Darkness tore through her heart. Long talons ripped the flesh of her body as poison ran through her veins, burning her soul from her feeble body. Her screams carried through the small cottage, the room itself deafening with piercing cries.

The cottage fell silent. The first darts of blush-tinted light brushed the thatch. It slowly crept to the window, caressing the glass with the promise of a new day.

The crone stood watch over the room. The shadows had eased, settled back to the corners. And as small shards of morning light cast angled shapes upon the wooden floor, the room held a new feeling within its palms.

The crone stared intently at the figure upon the bed. The child now lay deathly still. The woollen blanket about her, torn and shredded by her own little hands. Her fingertips blood-stained, great gouges of flesh and wool beneath her nails. Her skin, smudged and slick with crimson streaks, as was the once white linen slip, which now clung in shreds.

Men were now in the lane yonder. Through the window came their spiteful blasphemy—hateful claims of the devil's doings.

A thud befell the door. There was no time to second think or question. The crone strode to the bed. Standing over the girl child, she placed a hand upon her forehead.

'Child?'

She lay perfectly still as death itself, all but the slight rise and fall of her chest.

'Child?' Gently, but firmer this time.

A second thud.

'Let us in, old woman. Thou will and must open this door!'

The child opened her eyes. They latched quickly to her grandmother's face.

She paled at them, her heart taken aback at the depth.

The girl smiled and grabbed the crone's skirt, crawling her way up her body 'til she sat. Her dark hair, knotted and wild as the winter wind, stuck to her cheeks.

The crone staggered back a step.

'Thou cower from me, Grandmother?'

The crone did not answer. Instead, stepping forward, placing a knee on the bed, she hastily grabbed the pillow from behind the child. She pressed it to her face, quickly thrusting her thin body back on the bed. Tiny legs thrashed, her thread-like arms whipping, as her nails dug deep into the crone's hands.

Another thud to the door.

A bellowed demand.

A smash to the window.

A stone hauled through the room, hitting the crone about her shoulder. She faltered, her grip slackening on the pillow, her knee slipped, and she fell to the floor. The girl lay motionless for a moment, her grandmother's heart gripped by fear and pain.

The pillow was flung to the floor as the small child arose from the bed. She swivelled her legs around and sat before the old woman.

'Thou cower?' The girl smiled, 'why are thou afraid?'

'Oh, child of mine own child.' The old woman lifted her hand to caress the girl's cheek, brushing hair from her face. She rubbed her arm. 'My dearest child, they come for thee. They hover at the door; they will not wait.'

The child's eyes softened; her head tilted with acceptance.

'Then I pray to a God that will no longer listen to my plea, that thee make haste and quicken this.' She pulled at the pillow, passing it to the old woman.

The last thud. Breaking glass.

Another rock. Larger, jagged, a razor-sharp flint thrust its way through the room, landing with a lethal smash at the girl's temple. Thick crimson spurts spattered the crone's face. The girl lay lifeless. Her eyes, wide and fixed, her mouth, slack.

'Open this door, old woman!'

Slowly, she walked to the door, placed her hand upon the wood, her mouth close to the slice of light between the frame. She spoke softly through the chink.

'I shall not be opening this door, this day, nor any other.' She stepped back to the bedroom. Taking hold of her grandchild's lifeless body, she sat cradling the girl. She rocked her, stroking her little face.

'Then burn, witch.'

The rafters creaked as the thatch took hold. Great, leaping flames lapped at the walls. Billowing, grey smoke swirled the room as the shadows had done. The crone simply sat on the bed; her grandchild now safe in her arms.

Her face was resolute. She would not leave this world without leaving something behind—a gift.

> *'Darkness falls as hell does rise,*
> *haunting wisps beguile thine eyes.*
> *Vileness lurks within souls of man,*
> *as hearts does bleed and bodies burn.*
> *Mercy knows that evil masks,*
> *no solace does dwell in dark, vengeful hearts.*
> *The cursed man that brings forth the flame*
> *will know no peace or those with his name.'*

The crone spluttered; her lungs filled with blackening smoke. Her body charring in the growing flames. She did not falter nor cry. Instead, she thought of her children. Her girls that had played in the summer sunshine with hearts full of goodness and love. Their futures, full of hope and life. He had taken her children, one at a time, all in the name of his God and the righteousness of his misguided convictions. For what God would cause good healing women to drown or hang or burn.

She cursed the man that once was a boy, whom she had cared for when ill, had played within her yard. The boy, Matthew, who had once loved her daughter. But his heart now blackened with fear and misjudgment. The man that now, with self-righteousness, titles himself Witchfinder.

'I curse thee Matthew Hopkins and all your descendants. Burn in hell.'

Chapter Twenty-One

'For treachery comes knocking.'

Smouldering, brittle timbers crunched beneath his boots. It was gone. Nothing left. Hopkins trudged amid the embers of what once was, bitterly, his chest engulfed in sorrow. It would pass. He knew his return would, perhaps, bring danger to those he once loved, who once loved him.

A distant fragment of his existence, he had buried, along with betrayal and shame. For he knew, all too well, that it was his. The guilt lay solely at his feet. And now, those guilty feet stood at the perished threshold of his once heart's home.

'The body. The old woman, she must be buried, see to it.' He waved his hand to the lad. 'No!' he shook his head, removing his hat, ran his hand through his hair. 'No, send for the undertaker; I shall see to it myself.'

The lad, boy, no more than a youth, looked at the man, his brow furrowed. 'Sorry, Sir?'

'What are thee, dumb, boy?'

'Sorry, Sir, I only meant both?'

'Both?' Hopkins asked.

'Both bodies, Sir,' the boy mumbled. 'My Master, he says, there were two, Sir.'

'Enough of this, get me thy Master, bring him now.'

With that, the lad scurried off, stumbling over the debris. Leaving what remained of the smouldering cottage behind him as it leaked black smoke into the evening sky.

Hopkins stepped back from the charring mass to rest against the low stone wall. It was cold. The night drawing in around his shoulders and with it a chill.

His heart and mind fought. The child had died. He had been told so. Along with so many, she had perished from the fever. What other body could there be? The crone had become reclusive; she had been watched, no one left, no one visited. These past months, the cottage had become almost dead itself.

He sat, watching the glowing orange veins thread through what was left of the timbers. Remnants of what once was furniture lay broken, fractured, scorched, beneath great, lumbering, hunks of wooden joists. Only the outer stonework, in its crumbling state, marked the boundary of the cottage walls.

There had been moments, small sparks of deliberation, where he considered, his heart urged, to step foot beyond the boundary, to see, to speak, of a life he once knew. To see for himself, allow his own eyes the acknowledgement that the child was dead.

A ridiculous notion, one that would only bring pain, memories, the last of which had been successfully buried, had crumbled and burned along with the cottage. All were dead. Nothing left, nought of the kin he once knew. All had perished. Some by his own hand, ones he had loved the most, by his own hand.

The irony did not pass him by. He was revered, not liked, but crucial to those who employed. He was sought, engaged, to carry out God's work. His father's work.

Yet, to those he had loved the most, he was loathed. He had become his own breed of evil. He was the devil himself.

Chapter Twenty-Two

'Fear not, I'll keep thy secrets safe.'

Manningtree - May 1635

Throwing her blanket off, her bare feet hit the floor. Panting, hands gripping her hair, small fingers winding the strands around her knuckles 'til they stung. Her mind whirled, poor heart thundering beneath her ribs.

She pressed a hand to her breast, pushing hard to stop her heart from jumping so. It always hurt when it beat too fast. She wanted to weep, could feel her eyes tear. Biting her lip, she blinked them away.

Looking over to her sister, her outline and shape, barely visible, the room was dark. Straining her ears, she listened, concentrating on her sister's breathing. It was steady and comforting; she was still asleep. She wanted to wake her. She needed to wake her, had been told to. She had said so if this were to happen again. And, again, it had. But fear was coursing its path. Once again, mapping its way through her body.

She could not understand; she had been in her bed, then found herself flying, she knew, was sure as her heartbeat, she had been soaring above the fields. Had felt the leaves betwixt her fingertips as she reached the very top branches of the great oak. He had welcomed her, reaching his branches to greet her. She loved the oak tree; it warmed her.

She scuttled over to the window, ever so quietly pushing the stool, so it rested against the wall, just under the ledge.

Hitching her slip up over her knees, she clambered onto the seat, the wood was cool but smooth, and it too felt like home. It was mother's, she would not mind, so long as she were careful. Mother always scorned her for climbing. She must never climb, nor run, nor jump, nor play with the other children. Those children sniggered and teased her; they called her names. Mother said they were jealous of her beauty, but their words were cruel. She knew she was different, older than those others, turning fifteen on her next birthday. She had some understanding that she was a little simple; that is what they shouted at her.

She pulled her legs to her bust, tucking her knees under her chin and wrapping her arms around tightly. Wiggling her toes, her heels resting on the wooden seat. She was cold, the night was chilly, the window let in a draught, it blew its greeting to her arms.

Beyond the cottage garden, beyond the lane, the field, the meadow, stood her friend, the great oak tree. She waved her hand; she always knew he could see her, his leaves swished in return. His giant branches reached out to welcome her like mother's arms did. He would always keep her safe.

When it happened, Mother had said that she must stay calm, breathe, and pray to the Goddess. There she was, hanging in the soot, black sky, she could see her, the Goddess. She was looking down at her through the window, its diamond lines slicing her like a cake. She liked cake, she liked mother's honey cake. She liked the moon; it was pretty tonight. It shimmered, full and bloated, swollen with its cycle. It would soon be a sliver, a crescent slice again. She did not much care for it then.

A wave of panic started in her toes. It travelled, crawling its way up her legs, her body until it reached her throat. She wanted to choke. She could not see. Trembling, her body hurt, a great pain in her chest, her heart thumping once more.

She wanted it to stop. Her fingertips grabbed the window ledge as her mind blackened, dizzy and dazed. She fell to the floor, crunching her thin body into a ball, hugging her knees to chest, and let muddled thoughts take her away.

It was black no more, nor was it night. It was light and morning. She stood by a gateway; a long winding path led to a house. She recognised it, though, had never travelled beyond the wall. Standing there now, hands gripping the flint stones, course beneath her palms, heart-pounding, and a feeling she could not quite fathom. Anticipation, eagerness, or was it fear, dread, that whispered.

'Twas the Minister's house.

Children lived here too, but she was never allowed to play with them. She would watch, though, from her tree. She would watch Matthew. She liked him, and he liked her; she was sure of it. He would talk to her, the others would not. His brothers never bothered with her, simply ignored her.

Yet, not her sister. All the Minister's children liked her sister. She was pretty and clever. Oh, so very clever, and kind too. Matthew liked her sister.

She would watch them sit beneath her oak tree, hands entwined, bodies close. Sometimes, they would spend long hours beneath the oak, sheltered by its great, leafy boughs that hung low, its twig fingers almost sweeping the long grass, hiding them.

She would listen, from up in the branches, she would climb, skinning her knees, to reach the highest, almost sitting among the clouds, up where the birds would play. She would lay there all day as her friend kept her secrets. He would never tell all he knew of what lay in her heart. Lately, she felt a strangeness, a warmth deep inside. Her belly would skip and twirl, almost to make her sick, but it was too nice, a peculiar sensation that made her smile and laugh, and oh so warm.

She wanted to tell someone of these notions, these odd feelings that made her body quake and heart miss a beat whenever she saw him. He was beautiful, like golden sunshine. Yet, who could she tell? Not mother, she would scorn her, for she was not meant to climb the oak tree.

Hence it remained secret, this new curiosity that struck her body with a great firebolt. In her private, leafy sanctuary, she would watch.

Daydream.

That it be her, he caressed, coursing his palms beneath her petticoats, 'til it made her squeal. Unlacing her corset, running his lips over her breasts. Pushing her onto her back as he lay over her. His body covering, 'til she dissolved into him. He would move, strange motions, softly at first, growing faster. Then a growl from deep within. A judder. Then life would stop. The entire world would halt, as if the Goddess had commanded it, no birdsong, nor rustling leaves, merely the thud of her heartbeat, deafening inside her skull, her fingers wet betwixt her thighs.

They never saw her, nor did they hear her soft sighing, but she heard theirs as the breeze carried it to her ears. It whispered betrayal. For she cherished her sister dearly, but she loved Matthew.

The stone wall sharp beneath her hands, she gripped and gazed up the pathway. He was inside; her heart jumped its odd rhythm at the thought of him, this night, asleep in his bed. Yet, the sun was warm on her arms. Looking down, she saw her slip. Why was she still in her night slip? Why was she not in her bed? Her mind began to wander until a cry. The sound, loud, coming from the house at the top of the path.

She took a small step forward, watching her bare feet as she did. The ground was dirty, dry, dusty. Mother would be cross for getting her feet filthy; she had no time to find her shoes now.

The cry again. Then, another sound, a man, a shout. What to do? She needed to tell mother. Mother could help; she could always make others better. The woman again, she was crying, louder now. It bellowed inside her poor skull, so loud it made her ears ache.

She began to run. The path, so long, she kept running, frequently looking back, the flint wall gradually disappearing behind her.

Run, get help.

Panting, she reached the house. It was bigger than their little cottage; the door stretched up so high she could not see the top. She pushed on the wood; it gave way to the hallway beyond.

Silence. No shouts, nor cries, nor wretched screams.

The young maiden stood on the threshold, neither in nor out, the sun hot on her back; keeping her grip on the door frame, she peered in.

'Hello.'

Her voice was minuscule, her word swallowed by the dark panelling.

'Please.'

Feeling the need to enter but the fear to do so, she kept calling. This would lead to no good, mother would scorn, and the Minister would have his say.

Oh, what to do?

With trembling legs, she carefully stepped from the sun's rays into the dark.

It felt murky, sombre; she did not want to go any further, remaining on the threshold. It felt wrong. Everything felt wrong. Like death.

Chapter Twenty-Three

'Cover your ears… and hide thy feet.'

Poor, simple girl, what could she do? She had no power nor knowledge to aid, help or comfort. She yelled, her lungs fit to burst and bleed, right here upon this cold, dank, death-filled place. Mother did not hear. Again, she yelled, atop of her lungs, she cried for help. No one came.

She was afraid.

The woman stood before her. Gleaming amid the wood panels. Her skin, pallid, white as her nightgown, her hair piled beneath her nightcap. But, oh, those eyes. Stark, wide, staring, no sign of sight. Glaring, boring, a great piercing hole through the young maiden's heart.

The white lady opened her mouth. A cavernous hole of nothingness, black and inky. Her face distorted, gaunt, dark sunken eyes, hollow cheeks.

A scream. For that is what it seemed, her eyes bulging, nostrils flared, lips taut and colourless, yet no sound—a silent cry.

With a timid step, the lady moved closer, her gown sweeping the floor; 'twas as if her feet were no more. She hovered, glided ever closer. Long, thin arms reaching forward, fingers stretched, thin skin barely covering her bony knuckles.

The maiden shook: she should not be here. She would be scolded for being so. Though in fear, her feet remained, planted, growing roots. Looking down, her bare toes began to blend, disappear, mingle as one with the floor, her ankles swallowed, as one with the wood.

The lady with her white glow reached forward with her fingertips lightly brushing the maiden's arms. Then her long fingernails grasped, sharp, scratching and snatched at the maiden's sleeves.

Chilled. Icy cold. She covered her face, clenching her eyes tight, her ears buzzing. The woman screamed, piercing her eardrums, knife-sharp pitch.

'I warned thee never to enter my house.'

†

Warm and damp, the cloth dabbed her brow. She drifted, her bed warm, soft. She wriggled her toes beneath the blankets. They were there; she was home. Though, she dared not open her eyes. Fear still lingered, behind her eyelids, the sight of such horrors, desperate, pleading, death itself.

'Be still now, child.' Her mother took her hand, resting, tucking it beneath the blanket. 'Sleep now, worry not.'

The young maiden drifted, her breathing slowed, shoulders relaxed, head calming into her pillow. Her mother watched, hesitant to steal her eye away, her poor child, her poor screaming, troubled child.

'Mother, this be the second this week.' Her eldest daughter stood behind, her hand upon her shoulder. 'What are we to do.'

'Thou will do nothing. No good will come of meddling.'

'It would not be meddling. Surely, I must tell Matthew, tell the Minister.'

'No.'

'He would not understand. They have no understanding, no knowledge of this. It will only instil panic, or worse, hatred and fear.'

'I cannot sit by and watch, knowing in my heart I did nothing.'

Standing, leaving the bedside, she guided her daughter to the door.

'Thy sister, she has a gift, but it could soon be seen as a curse. I will not have her seen as a threat.'

'She is not a threat. It is known by all that she be simple, of a simple nature.'

'But there are many who would see her visions, her dreams, as the devil's work. Think daughter, there is a history there; it may be seen as vengeful.'

'It is absurd.'

'But it be the truth. Ponder on the Minister's reaction. What is it he will say when thou explain? Think on last Winter, he will see it as a vengeful act, an untruth, but a spiteful act nevertheless.' Placing her hand to her daughter's cheek, she patted. 'Such a good girl, but do not be misled by feelings that sit in your heart.'

'Maybe to tell Matthew, though, Mother.'

'And, if it is to be true, then what? It will go from being childish spite to something much worse, a curse upon his household.'

'But Matthew, he be good and kind, he would not take my sister's words with anything other than concern. He cares for her.'

'Yes, 'tis true, he is not uncaring to her feelings. He has never tormented or had her play the fool, but please, do not mistake his kindness for understanding.' She kissed her daughter's forehead. 'Now, enough. No words will be spoken of tonight's episode. She will, for the most part, forget her dream, as is usual.'

The young woman watched her mother as she returned to her sister. Her poor sister, of such a sensitive nature. Her instincts were to protect, cradle, mollify from the world's woes. Of late, though, these dreams, visions, had increased, been plagued with fear and sorrow. She had watched her sister become more reclusive, with a reluctance to share her time and an eagerness to escape her company, to seek solace amongst the branches of the oak tree.

It troubled her. Knowing the change that occurred of late, that still lay thick in the air, an alteration in mood and body. She understood its power and impact, her own, a mere handful of seasons before. She had looked to the Goddess moon; she had played her part, had stepped in and made right of the confusion. In reflection, to the Goddess herself, as her cycle played parallel to her own.

Alas, with her sister, there was more.

Winter had seen the beginning, of what, she was not sure, but there had been an altercation. A few spat words of spite, hatred from Mistress Hopkins. The dog, their dog, had found a nasty, evil end, that was true. But she could not believe it was at the hand of her sister.

She was not so simple or a fool that she could take life. And that of a helpless pup, more absurd. Still, the sight of that puppy, hanging from its tail, blood dripping, soaking the snow masked ground, its throat cut from ear to ear. It haunted her dreams, still. But, most of all, the sight of all four of its severed paws that lay sprawled at the foot of the oak tree.

Mother had scorned, beaten, forbade her to leave the cottage. There had been words, she had given an apology, her innocence pleaded, she had been judged by the Minister and found her plea the truth. A rangy village youngster found to be the culprit.

Yet, now, as she looked upon the sight of her sleeping sister, a wave of fear hovered over her soul, for something new, that there be more than found, doubt niggled, nibbling at her guts, when she thought of it.

Chapter Twenty-Four

'For it's not what man will take…'

Cruel words spat from their lips. Senseless, foolish, dim-witted.

A rangy boy, legs thin like spindles, a youth between boy and man. An age to know better than to taunt. His eager words of spite spurred the others, who went from watching to gathering. They hurled, pelting a bombardment of firepower fit for stoning a wild animal rather than a simple girl.

She scarpered, running as fast as her legs would move, her petticoats hitched about her knees to hasten her escape. The meadow carried her legs through the long grass, swiftly taking to her safety. The great oak insight, a sharp intake of renewed breath filled her lungs, 'til her hand finally touched the bark. It warmed and soothed her as if taking her into its lumbering boughs.

Smash. Coursing through the low branches, sprawling fragmented foliage in its wake, it hit its target.

It lay heavy in her palm, the sharpest edge streaked with her own scarlet blood. She turned it over, flipping the sharp flint with her thumb, the sticky wet smudging her digits. Tentatively, her other hand went to her head, exploring through her long hair for the source. She found it, her hand wet, blood dribbling down her neck, puddling a little in the hollow of her collarbone.

Wondering if it was better to stay or move. To hide, here beneath the tree, or run for home, to mother, who would make better, mend her wound, console her pride. No, she would sit, await their leave, 'til it be safe to walk, for the notion of running filled her mind with dizzy thoughts.

She lay down, her back pressed hard against the ground, swallowed by the grass, lush about her figure. They would not find her here; she was sure of it.

Feet, heavy, fast.

The rhythmic thud travelled the earth beneath her head, juddering the ground, 'til those feet came to rest at her side. She wanted to open her eyes, felt she must, but her mind was roaming, the pain splitting.

A hand cradled her head, resting it upon something warm, steady. A cloth pressed hard against her wound, another mopping the bloody mess from her neck.

Her eyelids flickered, her eyes squinted against the sun, splintering through the tree above. A figure, someone she knew. A scent she recognised.

Matthew nestled her head in his lap as he pressed hard with his doublet to stem the flow of blood. It eased. She awoke slowly and opened her mouth to speak, her face quizzical at first, then, a smile.

'Hush, do not speak.'

She lay watching, his eyes, his face. Her thoughts went to her sister; a pang of something flashed in her breast, a twinge of shame, guilt? No matter, she blinked it away, and it skulked off to where she hid such feelings. Her thoughts were only of him.

'Matthew?'

'Thou are hurt, lie still, at least 'til the bleeding halts.'

'Please, Matthew.'

She pushed herself off his lap, her fingers within the grass as she sat up. Her bodice, wet through, stained, dark and bloody. In a panic, she began to rip it from her skin, tearing at the lacing, pulling at the ribbons, throwing them to the ground, thrashing limbs, discarding garments.

'Please, no.' He eagerly attempted to halt her hands, gripping her wrists. 'No, thou should not . . .'

He stared at her wide eyes, her clothes sprawled about the grass, pale skin naked, smeared with blood.

She grabbed his hand, plunging it up betwixt her thighs. He could find no words, struck dumb by her bizarre actions. However, he made no attempt to resist. She sat back down yet gripping his wrist, keeping his hand where she craved.

Staring, never taking her eyes from his, she grappled with his breeches, her inexperienced fingers wrestling with the buttons.

'No.'

'I know this is what thou wants.'

'No.' He could find no other words. An internal battle raged, his thoughts of her sister, but his body behaved at will.

'I have seen thee with my sister.'

'I love thy sister. This is wrong. Please, dress, and I shall escort thee home.'

She listened not, her thoughts on her needs. Achieving her goal, exposing his nakedness, she gaped at it. His skin smooth, taut, as it stood tall, rigid.

'I have seen what she does to thee. Please, Matthew.' Legs astride, she removed his hand, his fingers wet, yet her grip still agonisingly vice-like about his wrist, his hand almost senseless, white.

She sat, lowering herself onto him. Astonished, he sat rigid, both with fear and then a great wave of need. Pausing, her legs gripping his thighs.

'Please, this is wrong. We must not do this.'

'Oh, but I love thee, Matthew. Is that not how it should be?'

'I will not take thy virtue.'

'My virtue?'

'Your innocence.'

'But thou took my sisters.'

'I love her; we shall be joined.'

'Joined? Thou will marry my sister? Even though she keeps secrets from thee?'

As the statement left her lips, a primal, predatory glint flashed her eyes; she pushed down hard and screamed, pain shot through her, she pushed harder.

He should recoil, pick her up and cast her aside, his morality fighting a fierce battle.

Gradually, she began to move, thrusting her breasts to his face with each motion.

Between erratic breaths, he watched her face. She was indeed beautiful, like her sister, but a simplicity lingered there, where the intelligence of her years remained absent. Except, this was different; he looked upon her, viewing a new, animalistic need that shot through her stare. Though it petrified him, he could not help but pity. She may never know love, joining and children, as her sister would, a life of a woman. This young maiden was dammed to remain so, a child.

Her fingers gripped his shoulders, digging her nails through his shirt 'til they seeped blood from his skin. It stained the linen with its crimson tone. A yelp left his mouth as a wave of release left his body. Her body bucked, taking her moment, along with his. Burying her face in his shoulder, he could feel the quake of her tears. Her body began to shake. She wailed.

'Please, do not weep.'

Matthew pushed her from his lap. Falling, a heap to the warm grass, curling, hands about her face. He sat a moment, gathering his senses, fastening his buttons.

'She does not love thee.'

Her voice muffled; she wiped her nose with the back of her hand as she sat. Long strands of dark hair sticking to her wet face.

'We shall be joined this season next,' he assured, though his voice quaked with unease. She stared.

'My sister keeps a great secret from thee, Matthew. I have heard them speak of it, Mother and her. So many secrets, Matthew.'

'What possible secret could she be keeping? Thou are mistaken. I know thy sister's heart; whatever it is, it will be of no consequence. Please worry not . . .' Pausing, he knew the words must be said. A deep breath filled his lungs to give some credence to his tone. 'This, what we have done here, this day, it should never be spoken of, thou understand, that it be very wrong?' those words shook.

'I understand a lot of things, Matthew.'

His name sounded odd on her lips; her voice strained. He watched as she glared and stood. Her naked body bloomed in the midday sun; unable to remove his eyes, she smiled, reaching for her clothes. Slowly, she dressed, the garments now stiff, the blood, brown and sun-baked.

'And she loves thee not. I cannot understand how she can be so cruel to play with thee as she does.'

'Please, thou are mistaken, worry not. I will escort thee back to the lane, though I feel I should go no further. I need to run a few errands for my mother.'

'Thy mother?'

Matthew gazed with the question, what of his mother?

'Thy mother, Matthew?

'What?'

'I heard them speak of it. Yet another of the secrets she keeps from thee.'

'Please . . .' He stood, resting his hand on the tree; he reached over to her, gripping her hand. 'What of my mother? What is it?'

'Oh, Matthew.'

She looked at her hand resting in his; she liked the look of that. Is that not where her hand belonged, within that of whom she loved?

'Tell me.' His hand clenched firmer, she continued to stare. 'Tell me, I demand it.'

Those words shot an arrow through her chest, the harshness, his sharp tone; she shot a look equally as sharp, and her eyes flashed darkly.

'Thy mother, dear Matthew, is dead.'

'Dead?'

'She had no feet.'

Chapter Twenty-Five

'Watch thy feet… death is eager to take them.'

Matthew ran. His dusty boots thud the dry, dirty pathway to the door, he fell against it, pushing it with his shoulder, his heart hammering inside his ribcage.

Inside, the hallway offered its customary dark, oppressive greeting.

To find his mother was his only mission. Taking the steps, two a time, he made swift work of the staircase, reaching the gallery landing in mere moments. He glanced down over the wooden rail, the hallway below silent.

He called, his voice reverberating, bouncing from panel to panel, door to door. Waiting for a reply, he called again. The house remained hushed like a grave. Then his ears found it. It crept along the hallway to greet him, weeping. He ran.

The door flung open, his hand barely reaching it as his boot made the first contact. He kicked it with a loud thud, disturbing those within.

Matthew stood on the threshold, his hand clutching his hair, gripping in hope to yank away the sight before him.

'Father?'

The Minister knelt beside the bed. His hands pale against the black of his sleeve, clutched the hand of the bed's occupant. An oddly white figure, laying unnaturally twisted, still.

'She fell,' he whispered without turning to his son.

'Father?'

Matthew passed over the threshold with slow, tentative steps, his body captured by the dust motes as they cavorted through the gap in the drapes. The window viewed the glory of the spring day at odds with the dark, depressive tone of the room. Death lay thick on every surface.

'Her haste was too great. She fell.'

'I do not understand . . .'

'Gone.'

'Her feet?'

'What boy?' His father rubbed his wife's hand, turning his ashen face to his son.

'Father?'

'She fell the full length of the staircase, broke her neck. 'Twas as if someone took her feet from beneath her.'

Chapter Twenty-Six

'Take heed, for secrets swiftly fester.'

Matthew continued, not even a backwards glance; his step never wavered. He would not stop 'til he was as far from this God-forsaken place as his boots could carry him. The tree, he would make it to the oak, yet, as the thought seeped into his own private darkness, it has been tainted. She had tainted the tree. Death had tainted home.

'Matthew, please, I need to speak with thee.'

The voice was of his love. She called, he heard, but his feet continued as new guilt stung his skin with the remembrance of what had passed earlier this day. This day. It felt a lifetime of days, hours, moments had passed. His life destroyed.

'Matthew, please.'

Sighing, his feet came to rest, dry specks of dirt settling upon his leather boots. With gripped fists, he turned to see her running the length of the lane, the cottage disappearing behind her.

'Please, wait.' She panted as she reached his side, clasping his hand in hers. 'I saw thee walk my sister homeward earlier. The village children at play again, I see. Mother has bathed her wound. I needed to thank thee.'

Her words, breathless, rushed. His face blank, distant. 'Matthew? Whatever be wrong?'

'My mother?'

'I do not understand.'

'I spoke to thy sister.'

'Oh. I see. Did she explain, fully, for it is not as it seems, please do not blame her for it, she is but . . .' Her words fell short at the sight of his face, reddened, tear-stained. A pang of guilt shot across her face; he saw it. 'Matthew, thee must try to understand, she suffers from these dreams, visions, they are of an innocent mind. There is great confusion within her; they are but images. Please, do not take them as truth, only a concern,' she sighed, 'she means no harm; she is but a simple child.'

'No, see, that is where thou are so very wrong. Please do not ever assume or attempt to reassure me of thy sister's innocent musings.'

'Matthew. Do not ever talk of her in such a way. . . with such, scorn.'

'My mother, she spoke of her today, after . . . when I walked her home. She is dead.'

'Matthew, it was but a dream.'

'No.'

With lost vigour, his body slumped to the ground. He sat with his back nestling against a hedge, the sharp, twiggy branches spearing through his shirt sleeves. His breeches dirty, no doublet. His beauty abandoned, she watched as the sight of him confused her. He was but a slice of the man she loved. His wits torn, strewn to the ground, with the dry weeds.

'I ran home. She was right.'

She said nothing. There were no words, thoughts that she could share on the matter, none, but those she should have, yet, kept silent.

Darkness leached in around them. The usual light, the golden glow that surrounded their company, had disappeared, replaced with a deep blackness that spoke of death.

As she beheld his features, her heart now found deceit lurking beyond that beauty.

'My mother is dead, just as thy sister foretold.'

'Oh, Matthew.'

Taking his hand, she clutched it to her breast, kneeling in front of him, eager to find a speck of the boy she loved within that stranger's face.

'Matthew. There is something I need to tell thee.'

'One of those secrets, thou keep.' Glaring, his eyes cold, they smirked along with his lips as he spoke.

'Please, this be so very important,' she pleaded.

'First, my mother, what other dark, little secrets do thou keep from me. Sisters, as thou are, both deceiving, lying, whispering secrets. My mother is dead this day. My father now sees fit to send me away. I am to leave on the morrow, at sunup.'

'Leave?' panic whipped that word from her throat with a voice that trembled with pain. 'Thou cannot.'

'I am. I have no choice. He has found me a position within a small firm to study law. I can say that, after this day, I will not be sorry to leave this damned place. For wherever I look, it is tainted with deceit and lies.'

'Oh, Matthew.'

'Do not bleach mine ears with more lies or little secrets that thou keeps hidden. My mother. Think carefully before thou answer.'

'No, 'twas but a dream, Matthew . . . dreams, visions that is all. There are no secrets I keep.'

'And the blood we found at the oak tree?'

'Please, do not speak of this again.'

'Blood, thick, dripping . . . along with the paws that belong to our dog. And thy sister played no part in that either? Thou knows as well as I.'

'Matthew?'

'Cursed. I swear as God be my witness that something unearthly sits beneath the surface of thy sister. Perhaps thee as well.'

'What scorn is this, what hatred and hurt have spurred just spite from thee. I love thee, Matthew.'

'Perhaps, yes, I can see it now. My fate, of those I've loved, all lost by thy hand.'

His eyes fevered with turmoil, sharp as his tongue.

'I can see the darkness that sits behind thy beauty, and thy sister is the same. She looks with innocent eyes, thou plead her case of simpleness, foolishness. But she be no less than devious, taking what she seeks.'

'Matthew, I truly understand that thy heart is breaking. Thy poor mother.'

'My mother is dead. Thy sister, she cursed her, I am cursed, we are all but cursed. I shall never want to return to this damn place. There be nothing here but lies and wickedness, and I see it now. I cannot believe I have been so blind. Nothing but lies linger here. Maybe the gossip of thy kin be the truth.'

'I have given thee nothing but my love and truth. I have done nothing but love thee.'

'I am leaving and shall never return to this death-filled place.'

'Please, Matthew, I must tell thee, now, before it be too late.'

'What?'

'I am with child.'

Chapter Twenty-Seven

EAPI – East Anglia Paranormal Investigation
  'The Manningtree Account'
  Date: *31st October 2016*
  Location: *Mistley, Manningtree, Essex*
  Client: *Ms Dawn Cunningham*

Enquiry:

Initial contact made by the client's sister, Denise Cunningham, on 26th October 2016.

Ms Cunningham was given EAPI details by a friend of a friend; it's a tenuous lead, no recollection of name given. Have slight misgivings of the legitimacy of enquiry, hesitance in forthcoming details—appointment for investigation scheduled ASAP. No previous meeting wanted, the insistence that case is urgent. Not EAPI standard protocol.

Enquiry topic:

Suspected paranormal / spirit activity and disturbance at the above address. No further information was given.

Groundwork findings:

Generally, I've found all the readings from both the EMF (electromagnetic field) Reader and the Thermo (temperature) Reader were both normal. Slight misgivings on temperature readings in the dining room; however – conclusion, curtains had been closed keeping out sunlight. The rest of the house, all readings relatively normal.

Deduction - dining room was most active; the client confirmed our thoughts. The room has been shut up and unused for the past six weeks. Night vision camera was set up in the dining room to view the table as per usual.

Investigation Summary:

Séance held – attendees, Heather (spiritual medium), Dawn (client), Deni (sister), Maggie (mother) – Alex (myself) for observations, meter readings and notes.

Apparent contact made with spirit, the name given as Sarah and date of 1646. Apparently, a child, but no age, further dates or information gathered. Second, supposed spirit, but no name or dates were given.

High fluctuations on the Thermo Reader – both Dawn and Maggie showed extreme temperature increases. No cause could be found. Neither woman showed any lasting effects after the séance. References made by 'Sarah' to burning, with some mention of 'The General.'

(Note: Instantly, my thoughts were of the witch hunts during the mid-seventeenth century by the infamous Witchfinder General, Matthew Hopkins. His business was prevalent in Manningtree and surrounding areas from 1644 to 1647. With no surnames or further information gathered, I cannot identify the supposed spirits to any documented cases.)

Investigation notes:

As with most of our vigils, hysteria easily spread through the group. The supposed spirit 'Sarah' was forthcoming with regular activity, using the candle and client, Dawn, as a channel. All attendees experienced a 'breeze' around the table 'touching faces', as, with my preliminary findings, I could find no cause.

Meter readings were normal to begin. EMF readings fluctuated during high activity, as normal. Although, during the height of the séance, Thermo Readings were astronomical and off the scale—

reading exceedingly high temperatures for both Dawn and her mother, Maggie. Deni remained static throughout the investigation.

The appearance of a second, supposed spirit (no name given) seemed to possess Maggie, with references to 'Sarah' being a child. She gave no greater detail to investigate further. (Note: Maggie had seemed somewhat removed through the initial consultation and groundwork, only becoming animated during this part of the séance).

As with so many of these investigations, the alleged spirit 'Sarah' became agitated and frantic. Poltergeist activity heightened with the thrashing of cupboard doors, throwing of objects, whipping of curtains. Heather seemed to pass out or fainted at one point during the séance; it took her a while to gather her bearings. (Note: This, although not completely unheard of, did cause me concern, as she seemed to be out for several minutes.)

Activities eventually calmed. All readings returned to normal as the room calmed. Spirit activity seemed to have ceased. The room was in devastation, with broken belongings and furniture. We concluded all 'normal', gathering our equipment.

Our leaving was halted with the unforeseen return of activity. Resulting in me breaking down the front door to gain access as the family was trapped. The door seemed to have locked itself.

On returning inside, the lights were out, and we found Dawn, supposedly possessed by the spirit of Sarah once again. She was sitting on the floor in the corner of the dining room. The spirit was extremely aggressive, seemingly thrashing Dawn about the place. Heather's routine 'movement to the spirit world' had no effect. The spirit became increasingly volatile—Heather resorted to her 'Exorcism Prayer'.

Important: I add here that everything was normal, as expected when we left. Dawn had recovered after her ordeal, with no serious injuries—bruises and grazes to arms and knees. We both checked with Deni and Maggie, and all seemed coherent and understanding of the evening, with all thoughts that the supposed entities had left the house. Both Heather and I left the house that night at 23.50, adamant that it was safe to do so. Heather had consulted her spirit guide, Angelina, who had also confirmed that the entity had passed over.

The investigation concluded.

Personal Notes:

These notes are not official EAPI documentations. These notes are my own observations and evidence of my own experience of the evening. I hasten to add that this is NOT from my professional, scientific viewpoint, as I feel it cannot explain what I experienced. But is a personal account as an eyewitness.

What happened after was unprecedented in my 19 years of working within the paranormal field.

At 2.15 am, Heather received a direct call from Deni. She was in great distress and requested a revisit immediately. She gave little detail, only that it was urgent.

We arrived back at the said address in Mistley at 3.30 am. The house was as we left it, the door broken and ajar. Inside, the house was dark and silent. No sign of anyone at all. After quickly deducing that none of the lights were working, we checked the dining room before making our way into the kitchen extension. There were no signs of any of the women, despite clearly hearing crying, coming from what seemed to be the pantry in the kitchen. We checked the pantry, but no evidence of anyone or anything that could have made the sound. I made my way upstairs to investigate further in the dark, whilst Heather remained downstairs.

I saw no reason to think that either of us was in danger. We only wanted to find the women and to deduce what was the cause for the urgency.

I found my way upstairs with the little light from the downstairs hall. Once on the upstairs landing, I tried to gather my bearings and listened for the crying sound we had heard. I found a door, but on opening it, I only found the airing cupboard. Then, remembering I had my mobile phone, I used it as a torch. I made my way to an open door at the end of the hallway. Whilst in the hallway, however, I had briefly spoken to Heather downstairs. She had called up to see if I was okay after stubbing my foot on the cupboard door. I called down to her to stay where she was. I had no reason to think she was in danger.

It was the last time I spoke to her.

I made my way to the bedroom with the aid of my phone. The room, however, did have some light coming through the window from the streetlight outside. The curtains were open, and I could just about get an impression of the room's layout. At this point, I noticed a woman I assumed to be Dawn, crouching in the corner of the room, between a bedside table and the wall under the window. I assumed it had been her crying. I made my way around the bed to see her.

The huddled figure was wearing pyjamas. She was in great distress, with her head down and arms about her knees. She was shaking and crying. I repeatedly asked where the others were, her sister and mother. She didn't answer. It was at this point I heard a sound from downstairs. It's sounded like loud scraping, maybe moving furniture. I wanted to get down to Heather. To be honest, I didn't know what else to do, apart from getting Heather and getting out. I managed to pull Dawn to her feet. Again, I asked what had happened and the whereabouts of the others. It was at this point that my whole world turned on its head.

I looked directly into Dawn's eyes, but as she spoke to me, I became quickly aware that it wasn't Dawn I was talking to, but Sarah. Never, in all my years working with the paranormal, have I ever encountered evidence or witnessed anything that I deemed as proof of the spirit world. Any witness account where a logical explanation could not be found. But now, I honestly have no idea. What I witnessed that night would stay with me always. As I looked at Dawn's face, the spirit, the entity, the ghost, whatever you want to call it, was talking through her. I have no doubt in my heart that it was the essence of Sarah. I am fully aware many will dispute that, that it was my fear and tiredness taking their toll, and it could all be explained away with hysteria. I have myself in the past used the same explanation.

I wanted to get out of that room as quickly as I could. I tried to entice Sarah to come downstairs so we could find Heather. It was at this point that she became agitated, her movements and body language jerky, she became lucid. Dawn turned to me, and in her voice so I know she was fully aware at that point, expressed that we should be quick before they came back.

Whoever they were.

I dragged Dawn around the bed, getting to the door. I was almost there when she pulled me back. Sarah, again. I felt lost. She made me sit down. I have no explanation of why or how I felt so compelled, but I had no choice, and I indeed sat down on the bed. I saw in her eyes a new playful expression, 'play with me' I couldn't take my eyes off her face, but she looked past me.

I knew someone, one of the others, stood behind me. I couldn't make out who she was; I tried my hardest to look, but my head was fixed. I felt paralysed. Whoever she was, she had her own voice, and when I say that, it wasn't the voice of Deni or Maggie, although, of course, it was one of their bodies. Her voice was beautiful. That was my first thought as if she were flirting with me, playing with me; she came across as sexual and sensual. She whispered in my ear; I could feel her tongue on my cheek. My instincts made me want to retch, but, and I'm ashamed to admit it, for a moment, a very short moment, I wanted her. She aroused me. There was something about her tone and the words she used that stirred something inside me, and I had no control.

Then it came, a great walloping bang to my head. At that time, I didn't realise what had happened. It wasn't until I awoke, a while later, cramped in the bottom of the airing cupboard, with a great thumping headache. I hauled myself out of the cupboard, made my *way to the stairs, but before I could take a step, I tripped and fell down the whole staircase. I found myself a painful mess at the bottom. Not only did I have a very sore head, but I had seriously damaged my knee too. I eventually made it to my feet and the kitchen door. It was shut, I tried the handle, but it wouldn't budge. I was consumed with fear and worry for Heather, so I made a run at the door and found myself again in a heap on the floor. The kitchen was dark, of course, but I could hear noises and voices. My phone had taken the brunt and was now cracked, but at least it still gave me some light; I waved it around to see. The women, all three of them, were there. But I couldn't see Heather. To be honest, I didn't really care about anyone else or any of those spirits now. I just wanted to find Heather and get out.*

One of them spoke to me. It was a new voice. It wasn't Sarah, and it wasn't the other from the bedroom. The thought of her made me shudder then; I think I felt ashamed.

This new voice made me sit down. When I say made. I literally mean, just as before, with the spirit of Sarah in the bedroom, I had no choice. I couldn't help myself. She compelled me to sit down. So, I found myself at the kitchen island, with all three women in front of me. Deni glowered at me; she spoke more harshly than the others, like she meant business. I looked at Maggie; her eyes were soft and gentle on mine. I felt that pull in my stomach. Inside I winced at that longing.

I needed to find Heather. But instead, I found darkness again. This time I felt a hand on my mouth. And I must have blacked out.

I pause here as I try to gather the information before me.

Since that night, I have done extensive research on both the Manningtree area and the Witchfinder General, Matthew Hopkins. Although, as I have stated in the official investigation findings, without some hard evidence of full names, dates and details, I cannot verify the women's story. I do, however, believe that these poor souls were subjected, as were so many, reportedly around 230 in East Anglia from 1644 - 1647, to cruel torture and inevitable death at the hand of The General and his posse. These women were usually local healers, 'cunning women'. It seemed to be a precarious time to live. His practice was hanging, so the method of burning that he apparently bestowed upon these women is unusual. Despite most thoughts of witch-hunting, conjuring up scenes of burning at the stake, and as it had been commonly practiced in the sixteenth century.

I add here that this research has taken much of my time. I admit that it has become somewhat of an obsession of mine since I closed EAPI.

I hesitate to continue.

That night will forever haunt me. I regained consciousness in the middle of the street outside the house. It was still dark, but sunup couldn't have been far off. I wasn't sure what time it was. My head was hazy at best. I had no bearings for several seconds until I took a full breath. I looked up to see flames. I was lying on the footpath. I hasten to add; I have no memory of how I got there. I looked around eagerly, but there was no one about. It must have been very early. The house was on fire.

My instincts were to get help, call the emergency services. But I am so ashamed and confused to admit that I walked very slowly to the foot of the garden wall; I wanted to walk straight back inside that burning house.

I have no honest recollection of how long I stood, leaning on that garden wall. I felt mesmerised by the flames. I honestly shudder now with pain at the thought of my actions.

I felt a hand on my shoulder, I must have been shaking as it guided me away somewhere down the street, and I was sat back down on the pavement. I had no thoughts in my head. I can't explain the feeling of emptiness, and I wasn't sure what was missing. I must have been sat there a few minutes when I noticed people, noises, and sirens. The Fire Brigade had arrived. Someone had called them. I sat watching as yellow jackets and helmets scurried with ladders and hoses. Voices shouted and ordered. I just *sat. What sort of man just sits, but as those minutes passed, I had no real idea where I was?*

Or why I was there.

A glass of water was thrust into my hand, and a woman's voice ordered me to drink, so I did.

I had a blanket around my shoulders, and I was now sitting in the back of a vehicle; the doors were open either side of me, and the road was hard beneath my feet. It made my legs shake. A voice asked my name. I sat thinking. Then, I sat looking at the flames. I knew there was something important, but I couldn't gather my wits together enough to make sense of the puzzle. Again, the order to drink. Again, I did as I was instructed. Then a hand pulled up my sleeve, something tight around my arm, then it released, then a voice and some numbers. A light in my eyes and a hand on my forehead. Then, something cold to my chest and my back. Again, a voice, she told me to stay there. She said I was fine.

The sun was high now, and I could hear the flames. There was a lot of noise. There were a lot of people standing on the other side of the street. Two fire engines now, two great vivid eyesores parked centrally in this quiet little street. The fire was thick and consuming. A guy approached me, stood close; his eyes were wide.

What was my name? Had I been in the house? Did I know if there was anyone in there?

I sat there with a thick head. I couldn't think what the hell I was doing there. Then it hit me, Heather. The only word that left my lips was Heather. I remember his expression of complete frustration, but it softened with sympathy. Still, I sat there and kept repeating her name. I bashed my head with my fist. I remember throwing the glass on the floor and trying to get up. My legs were heavy, and although I tried to run, I kept slipping as my legs kept crumbling.

A hand came up to my chest to stop me in my tracks. The same fireman. He stood looking at me; I couldn't deduce his expression. The house behind him was a dark, charring mass, smouldering and hissing. The flames had eased, and huge clouds of grey smoke were finally dying down. I had no idea how long it had been. One part of me thought I must have been watching the flames for days. The other part of me said it was only seconds ago I awoke on the path.

My hand reached for my back pocket. My mobile phone. I hunted around, but I couldn't find it. I reached into my inside jacket pocket, nothing until my hand found something. I pulled out a card, a black business card. The guy took it from my fingers and read it aloud. EAPI Paranormal Investigations. He looked at me quizzically and continued reading Alex Rampling.

I nodded and confirmed that it was me. It came to me then, at that precise moment, as if my name was a trigger. I know that sounds utterly ridiculous, but I can honestly say that my name was like a sweep of lucidity.

I answered him with renewed clarity. Yes, I'm Alex Rampling. I'm a parapsychologist. I explained I'd been investigating paranormal activity at the house the night before, as requested by the resident. Then, Heather, the thought of her hit me. Oh, effing hell. Heather. I was told they were doing what they could. What did that mean?

I was sat back down again as a police officer came over to talk to me. Asked me no end of questions, some of which were pointless, I kept explaining, going over old ground, again and again, the séance, leaving all perfectly fine and driving home. How did I get back here this morning? I had no idea, and my head was banging now. I had a mother of all headaches, and my knee was giving me awful pain, which I had only just noticed. The officer, I know he was only doing his job, kept going over all the details. Obviously, he didn't believe it. Clearly, he was a sceptic, me too, I thought. Then I remembered the last minutes in that house.

Heather? I yelled. I remember everyone looking at me; I must have shouted over the noise. I needed to find Heather and the others. What about the girls, Dawn, Deni and their mother, Maggie? The *officer put his hand on my shoulder, which now bloody ached too. He walked away to talk to someone.*

He finally returned with the fireman I had spoken to earlier. They both seemed to scrutinise my face. For a moment, I felt guilty of something. But what had I done? The police officer looked sombre. I will always remember his expression.

Then he spoke. He needed me to identify a body.

I couldn't think what he meant for a minute. What did that mean? I remember asking him to repeat it. So, he did. They had found the body of a woman inside the house, and as I was in the house last night, could I please identify the woman's body.

A policewoman appeared from nowhere or nowhere I had seen. She slipped her arm through mine, and I followed the uniforms over to the side of the street. I looked back up at the house then, I could see the dining room, the window was black, tarred with smoke, the door wasn't there, not just broken but burnt to a cinder.

I looked at the path; another officer stood beside something lying on the ground. It was covered in a blanket; it smelt. Everything smelt. Everything smelled of heat, and something else that I can't, still, to this day, rid my nose of.

The guarding officer nodded and crouched. Instinctively, I did the same.

Wait. I needed to get myself ready for this. If this were poor Dawn, how awful this would be for her sister or mother. That is the only thought that kept going through my banging head. The officer nodded again and asked if I was ready. I nodded. I didn't see there was little else I could do. So, he pulled the blanket back.

Someone, I have no idea who, but one of them kept asking me. Again, and again. But I couldn't move my eyes. The body was dark, thick with smoke, blistered, charred.

It was strange. I remember that feeling in my chest. I sat beside her then. I felt the female officer's hand on my shoulder as she stood close by. I remember looking down at her shoes by my knee.

They asked me for a name. I asked about the others. But they didn't answer me. They kept asking me the same thing. Can you name this woman? But, what about the others? I kept repeating myself.

The female officer crouched beside me. She patted my shoulder. I looked at her. She was blonde. I looked back at the dark-haired body. Then back to the blonde officer.

We need to know if you can identify her, please. Do you know her name?

But, first, what about the other women? I needed to know.

She just looked puzzled.

There were no other bodies, she said. The house had been semi-derelict and boarded up for years.

I can only begin to describe my confusion.

Her name? They kept repeating.

It left my lips in disbelief.

Her name is Heather Hopkins.

Chapter Twenty-Eight

Suffolk - April 2017

Old tomes, files, ledgers, an array of paperwork scattered and buried the large desk, the dark wood no longer visible. Laptop perched on the edge; his fingers hastily tapped the last of the account.

The simple act of typing her name sent a new sensation through him, not just of pain but of not knowing. It still lingered there, his lost thoughts, his lost hours.

A long swig, then the heavy tumbler sloshed its golden contents as he plonked it back down hard. Missing the coaster, it toppled, splashing sticky brandy. Thick drops slowly soaked into the fine weave of vellum.

'Fuck it!'

Alex grabbed the glass and flung it across the desk. His fingers scrabbled at the documents. He wiped the paper on his jeans; the denim soaked up the alcohol. Drowsily, gazed at it, squinting, the ink still intact, his racing heart eased a little.

No matter how many times he had read the document, the sentiment, the meaning, the logic, no, there was no logic, nothing, none of it seemed natural, it was not real, this was not happening.

He was still consumed by the nightmare. He never slept. He was never sober. His constant state of drunken oblivion was his new welcomed state of consciousness.

Seven long months had passed. Seven months of slow acclimatisation, to what, he was still unsure. This new existence was nothing of the sort, for the thought of existing was to live.

He had closed the business; he had just taken down the website. It had not been a conscious decision, but nothing in life was conscious now. Alex, the rational parapsychologist, was gone. In his place was a numb shell, haunted day and night, not that there was a distinct difference between the hours by her memory.

She was there, with him; even now, he could feel her, sense her breathing. Hear her voice in his head. Feel her hand on his shoulder, on his face. When he slept, she was there, in his dreams, or was he still awake? Did he ever sleep? He could never tell. The brandy saw to that; it was his anaesthetic to keep blame in the forefront of his thoughts without dealing with the real world.

Dealing with the matters of solicitors, the will and headstones, that would draw a line beneath her memory to admit her departure. To commit her memory, along with her charred remains, to the cold earth, that would be to concede she was gone. How could he let her go when she was sitting, perched, on the desk beside him?

That is where she resided, watching over his work, listening to his findings.

A ringing, the phone, or mobile, his mind couldn't fathom which. His fumbling hands scanned over the papers, toppling piles of books to the floor.

'Oh, for fuck's sake.'

He stood up, staggered over to the window ledge where his Samsung lay in the moon glow. Grabbing it, holding it up close to his face to decipher the number. Nobody, well, nobody he wanted to talk to. He swiped the cracked screen to dismiss the call. And threw it across the room, hitting the bookcase, it fell to the floor in smithereens. Stumbling, falling to his knees, he attempted to gather the pieces, shoving the bits on a shelf.

He held his head in his hands, easing the aching in his temples, his throbbing skull. Watching his feet as he walked, he sank back into the leather chair, head-spinning on his shoulders, as he stretched across to recover the glass. The chair swivelled as he reached over to the filing cabinet and snatched at the crystal decanter. He mused at it a moment, the strangeness of its presence in his office, then, without another thought, drained it of its last drop.

'I know,' he muttered, his words slurred, 'You're moaning at me; I can hear you.' He tapped his temple with the glass, the brandy sloshing. 'I can hear you inside my bloody head. You shouldn't be drinking; why the hell are you drinking brandy? You never drink bloody spirits!'

He guzzled, taking the whole amount in one mouthful. Holding it there a moment, allowing the alcohol to burn the inside of his cheeks, then swallowed. It warmed his throat. 'Well, you're not bloody here to tell me not to, are you!' He closed his eyes and slammed the glass down, hitting the laptop; it toppled off and lay empty on the floor. 'No, you are not here. And why is that? Well . . . let me tell you why that is, shall I? You are not here because of me. It's my fucking fault, now, isn't it? So, I shall drink your bloody brandy if I want to.'

He crumpled in the chair, his head heavy on the sweeping back, the leather consoling his drunkenness, as his mind tripped and tumbled over his thoughts.

The lamp flashed, crackled, hissed and went out. Gone.

'Oh, for bloody fucking hell's sake, what now.' Heaving up from the chair, he reached over to the desk lamp, the bulb, hot to the touch, burnt as he wiggled it in the fitting. 'Fucking bulb!'

Barely upright, his legs carried him to the doorway, flicking the light switch. Nothing, no lights, no electricity, no power, the room was dark. Fumbling in his pocket for his phone, the seeping recollection of its broken state put paid to that idea.

'Fucking power cut! Ok, I can do this. Candles, where are the effing candles.'

The kitchen window let in a pinpoint trickle of light; the moon, full and bloated, at least allowed him to search the drawers. One after another, he flung open, rummaging, riffling through with drunken numb hands.

'Bingo.'

Alex grappled with a box of kitchen matches and a couple of half-used taper candles, enough left in them to light the rest of the evening. After that, when he'd fallen asleep, he cared not. The heavens could swallow him whole, and he'd not care. Or would he sooner be welcome in hell? He snorted at the thought.

†

'Come with me. There is no happiness left inside. Or outside. Look, look at the sky, even the sky weeps at the memories.'

Alex lay, with his arms over his head, his eyes staring out into the night. Another night when he had no recollection of getting into bed. It was cold; the room was cold. The month had been wet, leaving its heavy dampness lingering through the cottage. Even the beams seemed clammy to touch. No sunlight, no warmth. The cottage was as miserable as his thoughts; it echoed his emotions with its cold, dismal condition.

He drifted in and out of sleep. Memories of conversations, where he couldn't quite gauge or recall if they had been real or not, whether they were now or long past. A muddled mind of thoughts and words, of images and feelings, of wants and desires. Those were the worst, dreams of longing.

Those were the dreams that haunted the very pit of his soul, that ripped his heart out through his mouth, shredding it on his teeth, as it left his body in splinters.

'Come with me, Alex.'

There was a lightness to her touch that lingered as it swept across his skin. A swift rise and fall of his chest, as his heartbeat just a little faster. Her hand, lingering on his navel, just before she ploughed down to what she wanted.

Wanted and took.

He lay still, glued, stitched to the sheet. He never wanted to move when she touched him; he always wanted more. She would take and leave, then oblivion would seep into his skull, a short reprieve from his waking agony.

Chapter Twenty-Nine

Alex rolled onto his back, covered his face with the duvet whilst the light attempted to seep into the room. It was early, maybe not even dawn; he didn't know, nor did he really care. He was drifting back from his state of slumbering stupor. He heard her breathing, her footsteps, soft in his ears. They echoed in his head.

'Leave me, please, just let me sleep. I don't want to do today. I don't want to do life today. I have nothing to get up for. So, for bloody hell's sake, piss off and let me sleep.'

Covering his ears, he rolled over his arms tightly around his sobering head.

She gently sat on the bed, her body next to his, her hand lightly running over his shape huddled beneath the duvet. He was awake; he knew he was, as that now familiar morning hangover kicked in, nausea and dry mouth that stung his chapped lips. But, while he lay stripped of alcohol, of dreams and of night, he could feel her, a weight on the bed, a body beside his. She felt real, and he hated it.

'Leave me alone, will you.'

'Oh, please.'

'Please, Heather, just leave me alone. No more.'

'Let me in. Let me in; it's cold.'

He couldn't open his eyes even if he dared. He didn't want to acknowledge the truth, that she wasn't there, that she was dead and buried and had been for seven months. He wanted to forget the funeral, the reading of the will, the memory of that night when he let her die.

'Alex, come, let me in. I'm cold out here; let me in.'

There were no words left to utter as his mind gave up; his now fully sober brain knew she was dead, so what if he allowed his heart to imagine. He pulled back the duvet; he felt her weight move in next to him. His eyes closed; he didn't want a reminder of reality or of his insanity. Instead, he went with it. Let his mind wander to all those unspoken conversations, all those times he should have told her how much he wanted her.

She brushed her arm along his; his chest was bare. She touched his skin; her fingers lingered on the patch of soft hair between his nipples. Her touch was cool and smooth. She eased the duvet up and slipped herself over, astride his body, pushing him on his back.

The realness caught his breath; he wanted to speak but found his voice mute. A slight moment of panic drew the breath from his lungs. He could feel it; he had no control. His body reacted to hers as she rose, taking him in her hand, stroking, and allowed herself to lower onto him. She pressed her legs a little harder to his body as she slowly moved, gaining momentum as she rode. Her sighs filled his ears. Clenching his eyes tightly, he allowed himself the luxury of her.

Wanting her, needing her, as he had done for so long, his love for her had now come to this. It brought a great wave of confusion and panic with the ecstasy. He had no choice as she pinned him to the bed. He dared not open his eyes. He couldn't bear the thought of reality, that he was still dreaming of her, as he had done so every night these long months. In this moment, Heather was real, and she was taking him. He feared that, upon opening his eyes, she would be just a memory.

She gripped his arms, digging her nails in a little too hard, drawing just a trickle of blood.

Her movements were getting stronger, more urgent; he knew she was close, the thought made his body nearly explode. For the first time, he allowed himself to reach out and touch. He gripped her buttocks, pushing her body down harder, pushing himself deep into her. Faster, she took what she wanted, her breath warm as she buried her head into his shoulder, her long hair about his face. He could smell her, feel the heat of her breath and the coolness of her skin.

He wanted to scream, to cry, to yell.

'Oh, fuck!'

The sweet release. A great wave of relief, ecstasy, showered him as the quick realisation drew panic through his pores. He opened his eyes, her dark hair a web over his face. He always loved her hair. He could hear her breathing, short and heavy in his ear, as she gripped him between her legs and threw her head back, her body arched, her breasts bare, glistening in the dawn light as he dared to look.

The duvet lay a muss around them, he watched, as her hands ran through her hair, head back, eyes closed. She moaned in delight as she slowed, her movements slight and gentle. One last time, he pushed up into her, she sighed. He reached up and squeezed her breasts, running his hand down to her stomach; her skin was translucent, with a glint of beaded sweat.

He smiled. He lay, gazing at the smoothness of her skin, the beauty of her body. He wanted more; he never wanted it to stop.

Slowly, her movements stilled, her breathing calmed. Her hair lay tousled about her shoulders, strands over her face. Alex pushed himself up on his elbow, reaching a hand up to smooth out her hair. She pulled him to her, wrapping her arms around him, holding him close.

'How?' he whispered; he needed to say something. 'How can this be real? I don't want to let you go.'

'Please, do not, ever, leave me.'

She squeezed tighter. His breath hitched; he tried to pull away. He was still inside her, felt a wave of panic, but then there was more as he felt himself stiffen again. She gripped a little tighter with her legs as she thrust down harder. He gasped; he had no control; she felt so strong. She pushed him back down, his head against the pillow. Again, she lay her body over his, kissing his neck, running her tongue over his ear. He was consumed.

It was building again. This time, he pushed her up, holding her arms, her breasts in front of him. He considered her face; her eyes were closed.

'Look at me?'

She whipped her long, dark hair from her face and stared into his eyes.

He felt his heart stop. His breath lingered in a cloud before his face as it left his lungs. She was beautiful.

He let go; every ounce of longing, of desire, left his body in a great wave that took his thoughts and whipped them into a great tornado of fear as reality struck his heart.

'I know what it is thou wants, what thou longs for.'

He wasn't sure if he wanted to move or just die.

'Thou will never leave me . . .'

Alex lay rigid, gaping, confused, fearful. He pushed her slightly off, stunned by how real, fleshy and warm her body was.

For a moment, nothing stirred, as if the world stopped revolving, as her hand snatched at his. She gripped tightly, caressing the back of his hand with her thumb. Relenting, she sat beside him, her legs crossed, her body naked, shimmering. She smiled, her vice-like grip pinning him to her. Then she let go, easing her hands from his. She ran her fingers through her hair, easing it over her shoulder as it covered a breast; she teased the ends, sweeping a finger over her nipple.

Alex cursed as his body reacted, despite the panic that marched under his skin, his damned body wanted.

'Maybe I can help you?'

'Oh, but thou has helped me. Thou lit a candle.'

Smiling, she stroked his chest, lingered, trailing her fingertips over his heart. She tapped.

'My dear sister, she never loved him as I did. He left me because of her. How could he have done such a thing?' She scowled.

'Look, I really think we should talk about this properly. Let me get dressed.' He looked at her body as his groin ached. He needed a drink. 'I definitely think you should get dressed.'

'Oh no, we should certainly stay right here.'

Alex shifted off the bed, one foot finding the floor, as with such speed, she clutched his chin. Gently, reaching forward, her breasts brushing his arm, she kissed his lips.

'What else was there for me to do? My dear sister had a little misfortune, a fall, just enough to make sure that the child she carried would never be. My child was the one that he would love. But then she took her as her own, my dear Sarah.'

She sighed, shaking her head, a slight pout and a frown.

'She spent the most part of ten long years telling me of how he would come and take my child. Imagine that the fear that the child thou bore, a child born of love, would be taken. I had no choice. I had to save my Sarah.

Her face dropped; her beauty hovered on the surface of something much darker, uglier beneath.

'Alas, they are no more. Thanks to thee, my dear Alex.' Kissing his lips, never taking her glare from his face, '. . . and thy dear Heather.'

Alex shuddered as her warm fingers caressed his stubble.

'Dear Heather, her demise was not of my doing.'

She dragged Alex back on the mattress, pushing him backwards, revealing, exposing his evident want, as the sheet fell, knotted, to the floor.

'Foolish child, simple girl,' she mocked, 'they were always thinking me such a fool.' She smiled, her wide beam devouring her beauty with a sweep of annoyance.

Sighing, with ease, she swung her legs over, straddled as before. A great look of contentment twitched the corners of her mouth.

'Dear Alex, it matters not. I am here now.'

She rubbed her thumb across his bottom lip, dragging her nail; a bead of blood swelled. She flicked her tongue as her teeth grazed his lips.

'Thou taste so sweet, like honey cake.' A hint of laughter caught in her throat. 'Thou will be my pet.'

THE END

Acknowledgements

Behind every book is a writer bleeding from their fingers to create something of note. But behind them is a support network who give time and expertise—all to steady the madness.

Firstly, my thanks go to my incredibly supportive husband, James, who is there with me every step of the way. I couldn't ask for a better wingman or someone to help me hide the bodies! A special thanks to James for the gorgeous new cover design and for putting up with my endless bombardment of ideas.

To the wonderful Kayleigh Kipling for her brilliant editing skills, I'm so lucky she knows how my brain works. Where would I be without her eagle eye, perspective, and attention to detail?

Thank you to you, the reader. I am forever grateful. If you enjoyed this book, please leave a review; they genuinely are the author's lifeline.

About the Author

Becky Wright is an author with a passion for Gothic literature, history, the supernatural and things that go bump in the night. As a child, nothing tantalised her senses as much as a good ghost story.

Blessed, she lives in the heart of the Suffolk countryside, surrounded by rolling green fields, picturesque timber-framed villages, country pubs and rural churches - and lots of haunted houses.

She is married with a young son, four grown-up children, and grandchildren. Family bonds and the intricate nature of relationships feature strongly in her books, using the emotions of her characters to lead their actions. Her writing tends to lean towards the dark side with her inherent fascination for the paranormal, Gothic and the macabre.

If you have enjoyed this book, please share your thoughts by leaving a book review where you purchased it. Each review is gratefully received.

For information on Becky's books, writing and updates, please go to her official website. You can also follow her across all social media platforms.

www.beckywrightauthor.com

Printed in Great Britain
by Amazon